(UN)Bury Your Gays

and Other Queer Tales

A collection by
Clinton W. Waters

ISBN-13: 9798372121317

CONTENTS

(UN)Bury Your Gays

A Queering of H.P. Lovecraft's
"Herbert West-Reanimator"

Of Daniel "Danny" Moreland, I can only speak
fondly. He was my closest companion. My champion.
My single greatest achievement. I'm writing this down
now, while it's on my mind, as it has been on my mind
for years, in an attempt to exorcize it. I know this is a
futile aim, and will likely only serve to endanger my
current status as unincarcerated. But, there is the hope it
will simply sit as a file on my computer and eventually
corrode and rot beyond recognition. The same fate that
will befall me one day. And you, for that matter.

It's hard to say where I should begin. I haven't spoken to Danny in years. Had hoped to see him at our 10 year reunion, but he didn't show. Instead I had to watch the same old cliques form in little knots of humanity, observing them all over the rim of my plastic punch cup. I had to sit through the unfurling of a banner with Judd Thomas's face, a (half-assed, in my opinion) slideshow of old photos from social sites that didn't exist any more. Emily Halstead, Judd's girlfriend once upon a time, took the stage and Miss America cry-talked her way through a very special announcement. Miskatonic University had created a scholarship in Judd's name, especially designed for athletes, who we all know have a very hard time finding funding. I looked around the old gym, the site of plenty of torments, usually at the hand of Judd Thomas or his ilk. There wasn't a dry eye in the place. Aside from mine, I suppose.

"Humphrey?" Stacy Ingram slurred in my direction when I tried to sidle my way out the side door. "Oh my God, you haven't grown an inch," she said, measuring the top of her head out to mine.

"Dr. West, now," I said without attempting a smile. She gave me a piteous "Wow!" and asked me what kind of doctor. I told her I wouldn't be of any help for whatever she had. I ducked out into the sticky night as she tried to process what I had said. I looked down at myself, my attempt at dressing nicely, in case Danny had decided to come.

A bee laid on the asphalt. I stooped down and it burst into a buzzing sound as it tried to fly, but only succeeded in spinning in a circle. Extending a finger down, it latched on with its thorny legs. I saw its long tongue unfurl to taste my sweat. Its body vibrated and an iridescent sheen of green flashed in its dark eyes.

I had failed in seeing one old friend, but it seemed I found another. Or at least maybe one of its descendants.

I went home that night and tried to find Danny online. No luck, as with the last hundred or so times I had done it, even with dummy accounts. He had blocked me from seeing him at one point, but it seemed he stopped posting around then as well. He didn't turn up in any of the obituaries. I thought about calling his mother, who still lives across the road from mine, but assumed that would be fruitless too. She had always found me to be a bit of a creep. Or so she told me the last time I tried reaching out. I remember her singing a different tune in the old days, but it didn't matter much now.

I dug through my old things from high school and found notebooks filled with our correspondence. The boys we liked. The teachers that despised us. It certainly wasn't easy being the only two (as far as we knew) queer kids in the building.

In a rare instance of cosmic kindness, fate brought us together in freshman year when he was the new kid at school. We instantaneously became attached at the hip. Danny's family had moved to the middle of nowhere from the exotic land of Indiana because of some trouble he had gotten into. The other kids teased him for his accent and the way he walked. Just as they teased me for the "baby fat" my mom assured me would go away (but never did), and the sissy way I did everything. From the moment I saw him, something in me knew something in him. We didn't have any other friends, didn't participate in any clubs. It was just me and Danny against the world. The small town world that wanted to snuff us out.

I had a crush on him through that first year. I did mortifying things like lingering touches and burning mix CDs with thinly veiled song choices. There was no way Danny didn't know, but he was kind. We kissed just the once in a romantic way. Our first experiment, you might say.

It was summer and we were in his above-ground pool after midnight, the lukewarm water the only reprieve from the thick air. Crickets and cicadas cried out in the night, covering our attempts at being quiet. Danny glided out to me, the moon's reflection rippling out around him. My heart was beating so hard I felt it in my ears.

"Have you ever kissed a boy?" he asked. He knew good and well I hadn't.

"No," I said matter of factly, fighting for air. I shivered as he drew close and draped his arms over my shoulders.

"Me either," Danny whispered, bringing his face close to mine. I smelled mouthwash, minty and astringent. "We can try it. If you want."

"Go for it," I said, squeezing my eyes shut. I don't know what I was so afraid of. I knew I wasn't straight. I'd like to think I was worried it would ruin our relationship, but it didn't seem possible. It would be like saying you're afraid of werewolves, or zombies.

Danny's lips touched mine and…nothing. My eyes flew open and saw his were still closed. My glasses were askew, pressed into my cheek by his. I wondered how long we were supposed to keep on. He pulled away and I gave him a queasy smile.

"That was fun," he said and my face became hot enough to bring the water to a boil. I blurted out that I didn't think I liked him like that. He sighed with relief and wrapped me up in a hug. He felt the exact same way.

From that point to our Senior year, it felt like we lived a few lifetimes. Danny gave me the strength to come out to my family (and handle the fallout). He showed me good art and bad movies. When my mind went dark, he helped me remember reasons to go on living. He was everything to me. I was waxing nostalgic, seeing all the many moments of tender happiness suspended in amber. Then I found the bottom of the box.

The memories scattered from my mind as I unearthed what I knew was lying in wait. At the very bottom of the box was a leatherbound journal, cracked and peeling, the initials H.W. embossed on the front. Some great-great uncle's madman ravings about the machinations of the body. That all life was as simple as the turning of a wheel that spun a million different gears in time.

I pried the musty tome open and the spine creaked and protested. The bottom-right corner was charred black, but a vast majority of the pages were still "legible." The frenzied cursive of someone a hundred years ago, and the staccato, jagged letters I had scribbled in the margins. Near the end was the terrible bee illustration I had painstakingly copied from a library book, surrounded by the appropriate symbols, the mundane and fanciful ingredients standing in line. Even my best penmanship was as arcane as the sigils I had pulled from elsewhere in the text.

I drug my fingers down the bee's back and felt the grooves I had made with the pen, trying so hard to be accurate. It looked like a fuzzy blob with six rays fanning out from its center. An old, familiar voice breathed into my ear and sent chills down my spine.

It all started with the bees. My obsession, Danny's patient involvement. Around that time, we were in our last year of high school, and there were these studies about Colony Collapse Disorder. While there are other pollinators, this had struck a terrible fear in me. Bees abandoning their hives to die in some far off field. The queen producing babies that would never be fed. It felt sad and mysterious. And obviously, a high school senior was going to solve the issue. I flung myself into the project, and Danny was there to help me do the homework I was ignoring. My first major breakthrough happened on Halloween.

The day Danny died.

"Look at this," Danny said, sneakily passing me his phone under our shared biology desk. I flipped his phone open to see a text. The contact was only listed as J. It said: "Tonight. The boat ramp." I backed out of the message to see what else they had been saying, but Danny snatched it back. "A girl has to keep some secrets," he said and batted his long eyelashes at me. I sighed and pushed my glasses up my nose, something he teased me to no end about. "Don't give me the glasses push," he whispered.

"So I guess this means you're not helping me with the bee experiment," I said, then bit the inside of my lip. I really shouldn't have said anything. He'd already helped me with my research, mixing the various ingredients in my mom's canning cellar. Danny didn't have to hold my hand through the entire thing…I just wondered if he didn't believe in me. Of course it was an outlandish premise. Bringing bees back to life. He had only ever shown unwavering optimism. I was being needy. But if he was bailing on it, that also meant he was bailing on our planned slasher double-feature.

"Oh, shit," he said, wide-eyed. The white skull face paint cracked near his lips as he frowned. "I'm so sorry!" he said, squeezing my arm. I felt like an asshole for making him feel bad.

"Don't sweat it," I said. I lowered the hockey mask that rested on my head and breathed heavily. "But you know what happens to teens having premarital sex." We made stabby motions at each other and snickered.

We were the only two in our grade to dress up for the high holiday. But that wasn't anything new. We were Halloween people in a sea of popped collars and sweatpants with words on the ass.

The teacher, dressed as a green witch with a pointed black hat, snapped her fingers and told us to pay attention to the decades old nature documentary she was using to coast through the end of the day. We had all been eating candy since first period, so there was a general chaos she could barely contain. It irked me, as it usually did, that Judd Thomas could have his tongue down Emily Halstead's ear, but we were the ones causing a disturbance. He could plow into the side of the school in his too-loud muscle car and the teacher would ask if his mud flap titty girl decals were unscathed.

Case in point, Judd and his little cohort in the last few rows of the room were discussing how freaky we were. Judd, ever the paragon of Christian moral values, resorted to calling us satan worshippers. He was practicing for the day he'd take over his daddy's church. A crumpled ball of paper bounced off my head as I tried to tune them out. I opened it up to see a crude stick figure orgy between me, Danny and Satan. I showed it to Danny and he rolled his eyes. The urge to retaliate rose up in my throat, but knew it wouldn't do any good. Instead, a little ball of dread plunked into my stomach and weighed it down. Danny's, let's say nocturnal activities, wore on my nerves.

"Please be careful," I scratched into my notebook and slid it over to him.

"Don't worry!" he scribbled back. My mind raced with unsolved mysteries and tv exposes on the dangers of meeting up with strangers. He had gotten in the habit of meeting guys from personal ads online. Apparently our backwoods town was full of married men with secrets. I underlined my first message and drew a big circle around it. "I will mother :P" he wrote. I rolled my eyes. "Love you!!!!!!" he wrote with a dozen hearts. I leaned against him and placed my head on his shoulder. Being much taller than me, he had perfected craning his neck just so, so that his head would rest against mine. We had long ago mastered the art of staring ahead while others stared at us. I could still hear their thinly veiled whispers, but tried hard to concentrate on the movie as the teacher had asked.

"As is the end of all creatures' journeys on this planet," the scratchy canned voice of the narrator said from the scanlines dancing up the cathode rays, "our fox subject has perished." A sped up timelapse showed the fox riddled with flies and beetles, then maggots wore the flesh and fur away. A blip of color flew in and out of frame, a butterfly come to feast on the blood.

I traipsed through the woods behind my house. The McCoy farm, which was home to some beehives, was on the other side of a thin veil of trees. I was hunting for any bee that may have wandered from its home. With the severity of the disorder, surely even the McCoys' hives had been affected. The sun was low and my long shadow peeled away from those of the trees that stretched off into the fields. It smelled of cowshit and mold. The day had been warm, but the dying sun brought about a chill that annoyed me. I had forgotten a jacket and wasn't going to waste the last bit of daylight going back for one. I blew into my hands, which fogged up my glasses as I walked with purpose. My foot struck a large skull, maybe a deer's, nestled at the base of a stump.

I squatted down to inspect it, wiping the lenses of my glasses with my shirt. When I put them back on, I could clearly see a bee prying its way out of the skull's cavernous eye socket. The bee tumbled forward and landed amongst the leaves. It buzzed and flailed its limbs. I reached down to help it, but the legs slowed their sway. Eventually they drew themselves inward to the body of the bee and it was still. It was the first time I had ever watched something die with my own eyes. I had never been the bug smashing type, too "soft-hearted" my mom would say. I certainly didn't go hunting with my dad and my brother. To wantonly kill something felt needlessly cruel. But seeing the bee's spark fade into nothing, my heart ached in a peculiar way. It felt like something holy and secret. Like if my mom came looking for me and found me like this, I would feel ashamed. I gingerly picked it up and placed it in my palm. I ran a thumb along its furry abdomen, marveling at its softness.

The realization of my luck finally broke through my astonishment. I had no way of knowing for absolute certain it was dead, but I had to take the chance. The old journal with its brown stains had said the freshness of the specimen was tantamount. The best results would come immediately after life had ceased. H.W. had attempted the procedure with any number of creatures, but made no mention of insects. I didn't have the stomach to try a rabbit, or perish the thought, a cat or dog. But bees were important. Bees were an unseen pillar in the production of countless foods. I had to try, didn't I?

H.W. also benefited from a medical degree and access to syringes and sundry other medical supplies. I knew myself, though. Even if I had gotten my hands on a syringe, which were only used by diabetics and drug addicts in my town, I wouldn't use it to pierce into an animal, even a bug. Where would I even put the needle? I wondered. Instead, I would have to rely on my specimens ingesting the mixture. H.W. also had a diehard friend/assistant hybrid, but we all couldn't be so lucky.

Trying to keep my hand from trembling, I reached into my jeans pocket and pulled out a plastic vial with a screw cap. Though it is embarrassing to admit, all of my equipment, the vials and beakers and mixing rods, came from an amateur chemistry kit I'd gotten for Christmas years prior. While perhaps not the most sophisticated, they served their purpose quite well, as you'll find out.

My breath coming out in white wisps, I carefully unthreaded the top. The red rays of the setting sun caught the liquid and made it gleam and glimmer. Twilight washed over the forest in a hush, bare branches creaking and crying out. The fluid was fluorescent and green as I gently tipped the vial. A single bead of the concoction caught on the lip of the tube and then fell, splashing onto the bee's mouth. I couldn't be sure any of it had made it into the bee's body, but my elixir provided the only light. Tiny droplets ran down the bee's body and seemed to be soaked up into darkness. Straining my eyes, I tried desperately to stop my pounding heart, to try and feel if the bee was moving. I busied myself with resealing the tube, only a fraction of the mixture I brought with me used in the experiment.

Suddenly, the bee buzzed so loud it made me start. I nearly crushed it with a reflex of my hand. But I held my fingers out wide and I could feel the bee's leg's unfurling, grabbing onto the grooves of my fingertips and righting itself. It buzzed again and I had the strangest sensation of a buzz on my leg. I felt like an idiot when I realized it was the phone in my pocket. I pulled it out and flipped it open. I used the screen's light to inspect the bee. Its eyes shone emerald as the white light bathed it. The bee tested its wings, and before I could react, it flew off into the night. I stood there, dumbfounded for a moment. I had to tell Danny.

I looked at my phone and saw it had buzzed with a message from him. I opened it and saw a single word.

"Help"

I tore out of the woods, running towards the house. The door slammed open as I pushed into the kitchen from the backyard. "Humphrey West!" my mom scolded me.

"I need the van," I said, frantically searching for the keys.

"Honey, what's wrong?" my mom asked.

"You're not going out," my dad said from the dim living room.

"It's Danny," I said to my mom. "He needs my help."

"You're not going trick or treating with your fruity friend," my dad said, assuming because I didn't respond I hadn't heard him the first time. My mom took a turn scolding him.

"Humbug, if Danny needs help, you should tell his mother," my mom tried to reason. I waved her away in aggravation.

I grabbed my mom's purse. I pulled out everything and found the keys at the bottom. Before either of them could say anything else, I went back out the door and sprinted to the van. I backed out so fast it flung gravel up into the air. My dad appeared on the front porch, yelling, my mom's silhouette behind him. I ran over the jack-o-lanterns Danny and I had made and put at the end of the driveway. A few straggling families ushered their kids away from the road. I pulled out onto the road, smearing pumpkin flesh under the tires, and slammed the van into drive. It lurched and I stomped on the gas, leaving black tread marks on the blacktop. I only had my permit, but that wasn't going to stop me.

The boat ramp, the one people used for hooking up, was on the far side of the lake. I wasn't doing any hooking up, but Danny told me about it. I figured it had to be the one he had gone to to see "J". Like a fool, I was texting Danny as I flew over the hills and around the curves of the country backroads. I had sent him about a dozen by the time I slung the van onto a gravel access road. Going around a corner, I nearly had a head-on collision with a car that seemed to be driving just as recklessly away. Their headlights caused me to wince. As we swerved away from each other I recognized, without a doubt, decals of women in silhouette, reclining backwards, tits in the air.

I got to the boat ramp and slammed on the brakes, the van nearly sliding off over an embankment. Jumping out, I started to call Danny. Of course there was no reception, so the call kept dropping. I yelled out loud for him too. The dust cloud from my entry hung in the still air and burned my throat. I stumbled out into the darkness, calling his name between coughs and gasps for breath. My phone finally bleeped and began to ring. I stopped moving and heard the bright chimes of Danny's pop song ringtone. My trudging steps through the leaves sounded like gunshots, drowning out the singing phone. The call went to voicemail and I heard Danny say, "Sorry I missed your call!"

And at that moment, in the murky headlights of the van, I saw Danny's shoes sticking out from behind a tree. I ran over and used the flashlight on my phone. There was a mound of ruddy red-black leaves with two legs sticking out. I fell to my knees and shoved the leaves away. My hands found his shirt, absolutely drenched and clinging to his skin. Just as with the bee, in my flurry of movement, I couldn't be sure if his chest was moving. I felt upward, brushing away the dirt and detritus until I felt more cloth. I pointed the light directly at his face and saw it was covered by his hoodie. My fingers trembled as I grabbed hold of the hem and tugged it upward, terrified of what I might find underneath. It was being weighed down by his phone in the pocket, so I had to yank it up. I instinctively flinched away. I swallowed hard, my body knowing what I was going to see, my eyes already growing hot with tears. Forcing my head to turn back, his sallow skin shone in the darkness.

Danny's eyes were half-closed. The pupils remained large, unflinching in the light, staring up at the stars. His facepaint was smeared around his mouth and washed away at the edges, his skin the same white as the paint that remained. "Danny?" I asked, shaking him by his shoulders. He reeked of lake water. Just below his chin, dark purple marks seemed to be seared into the flesh of his neck. "Danny!" I shouted, smacking his face. "Please, Danny!" I screamed. A creature somewhere out in the darkness broke a twig as it scurried away. The flashlight turned off as I dialed 911. My thumb hovered over the green phone button. The green reminded me of my mixture in its little vial.

Surely it wasn't enough. But I had more back at the house. I just had to keep him from decomposing any more than he already had. Every second, more and more of his brain was becoming inert flesh, devoid of lightning. I pulled the tube from my pocket and leaned my back against the tree. A guttural sob left my body as I wrapped my arms around Danny's fragile ribcage, a macabre hug that made me retch, and pulled him upward. His head hung back at an uncanny angle that set my teeth on edge. I put his back against my chest so his head was resting against my shoulder.

My hands wouldn't stop shaking and were coated in the cold water clinging to Danny's clothes, so I couldn't get the cap unscrewed. I let out a grunt of frustration as I put the cap between my back teeth. I twisted the tube around and finally freed it from the seal. "It's gonna be okay," I whispered to Danny. "It works. I know it works." In the liquid's green glow, it seemed Danny's eyes were trained on me, watching to see what happened next. I tipped the vial onto his tongue and watched the liquid cascade down his throat. A small trickle dribbled from the corner of his mouth so I caught it with my finger and pushed it back up into his mouth.

I began rocking Danny. "I'll get you home. You can tell me all about it. We'll make sure that fucking asshole rots in jail forever." I'm not sure how long we stayed like this, but my teeth were chattering and a terrible shiver had set into my bones. In the sobering cold of the dark hours, I realized I was going to have to call 911. I would be a suspect, but it didn't matter. I knew what I saw. My parents would tell them I had stolen their van to go help Danny. Maybe that wouldn't help my story, but there was no sense worrying about it.

Danny's eyes fluttered, and I felt his eyelashes grazing my cheek. Something between a whimper and a laugh caught in my throat. I shouted his name a few times, but he still didn't respond. I felt my heart sinking to meet the rising bile in my throat. I brought my phone up, nearly touching his cheek. The phone's light showed that his eyes were slowly roving back and forth, as if he was dreaming. Better than nothing, I thought. The bark of the tree biting into my back, I slid upward, dragging Danny along with me. I pulled him backward through the gravel to the van, its headlights flickering out of life. Situating him in the front seat, I leaned over and turned the ignition. The engine struggled but hiccuped and sparked to life. Finally, my luck was looking up.

My family had gone to sleep by the time I got home. I killed the headlights and crept forward up the driveway. I saw a light was still on in Danny's house. Not to worry, Mrs. Moreland, I thought, I'll have your baby back to you in no time.

The moon was high and full, blazing white, watching as I pulled Danny from the van. Draping his arm over my shoulder, I staggered and we fell in the gravel. The rocks bit into my hands and I bit my tongue, wanting to shout "Fuck!" as loud as I could. Instead, I looped my arms under his and yanked him backwards in stuttering starts and stops. His feet clumped down the steps to the cellar, his sneakers thudding and squelching with the impact. I yanked on the chain for the single overhead bulb and it swayed, throwing our shadows onto the unfinished walls lined with jars of canned goods. As tenderly as I could, I layed Danny on his back on the table I had been using as a makeshift lab. I cleared my equipment away and was able to get him laid out flat. He was so tall his feet dangled off the end of the table.

"Sorry," I said to him as I tilted his head back and held his lower jaw open. His eyes still continued their slow journey from side to side. I went to the mini fridge and got out the full supply of the potion I had made. There was no more deluding myself. It wasn't a compound or a reagent. It was a magic potion. And it was going to bring my dead best friend back to life.

I had no idea on how to begin testing dosages. If it didn't take hold fast enough, I could waste it by giving him little doses. I pushed my glasses up my nose so aggressively the nose pieces dug into my skin. There was no other option. I would have to give him all of what I had. While I waited for it to work, I could make more, I reasoned. I stopped and smacked my cheek as hard as I could. This was insane. But I needed to keep my wits about me.

Getting a funnel from among my mom's canning supplies, I stuck the spout into Danny's mouth. I unscrewed the metal ring from the jar of ghastly green liquid and flipped off the cap with my thumb. "Bottoms up," I said and poured a slight stream down the side of the funnel. The plastic cone filled up as the fluid wasn't passing down into Danny's throat fast enough. I lifted his head as slowly as I could, straightening his neck out. The funnel let out a guttural glug as the liquid began to fall down into Danny. I held his head against my chest and watched the liquid swirl as it emptied out. I stood still, allowing every last drop to pass.

While I waited, I busied myself with peeling Danny's clothes from his clammy flesh. It wouldn't help the serum take effect to have his body extra cold from the water. I pulled his shirt over his head and down along his arms. I tugged at the soggy sneakers until they slipped free of his feet with a sick slurp. I undid the studded belt around his waist and slid his pants and underwear down and off his legs. I dug in a box in the corner and found an electric blanket we had once used when the barn cat had kittens. I draped it over him, plugged it in, and set it as high as it would go.

After all that, he had still not moved a muscle aside from his eyes. I pulled a chair up and sat at his head, getting a dry rag and mopping the water from his hair. I rubbed at the paint, slowly revealing his freckles, washing away what remained of the skull, hoping it would take death along with it. I rested my forehead against his and muttered little prayers. I knew if there was a God, he would not condone what I was doing. But didn't he also believe in vengeance? In justice and smiting of the wicked? He let his son come back to life, did he not?

A slow, whistly wheeze came from Danny's mouth and I shot up. His chest rose slowly, feeling like it took hours before falling back down again. Danny's eyes scrunched shut, then opened. He stared at the light bulb for a moment and I saw his pupils retract. I jumped up and shouted, throwing my chest down onto him in an embrace. "You're alive! You're alive!" I screamed, crying into the electric blanket that reeked of old blood.

"H-hey," Danny said, his voice a scratchy whisper. He brought a feeble arm out from under the blanket and patted my side. "Holy shit my throat hurts," he said. He smacked his lips together. "Why does my mouth taste like lake water?" His voice was muffled by my midsection. I leaned up.

"What do you remember?" I asked.

"Where am I?" he asked, shielding his eyes with his arm. "Why am I naked?" he said, lifting his head to look down at the blanket.

"You're in my cellar," I said. I went to the fridge and pulled out a bottle of water. He sat up and guzzled it down, the plastic crinkling as he drained it all in one go. "Do you really not remember anything?" I asked.

"No. We were in class. That's the last I remember. What time is it?" He began looking around, but the dank cellar held no clues. I checked my phone. Damn near dawn.

"Danny I need you to listen to me very carefully," I said, pulling the chair around to sit beside the table so we were facing one another. "Judd killed you."

"No he didn't," he said, shaking his head to the side, trying to get the water out. "If I'm dead, is this heaven?" he asked, gesturing to the musty cellar. I was too tired to humor him, but tried to keep my patience. "Or wait, it must be hell! We're sinners after all. Does that mean you're dead too?" He poked me in the chest and I smacked his hand away. I asked if he remembered my research with the bees.

"Well, yeah. It's all you've talked about for months," he said, giving me an exhausted smirk. I told him about bringing one back to life. About using the same method to bring him back to life too. The smile drained away from his face as I kept talking. "You sound crazy," he said and I could see fear behind his eyes. Fear that made me want to smash Judd's windpipe. Then bring him back and do it again.

"You were going to meet Judd, right?" I asked pointedly.

"You're not supposed to know that," he said. "Did we get drunk or something? My head is killing me."

"Being dead will do that to you," I said. Being a smartass wasn't going to help. But he wasn't getting it.

"I didn't see it happen. But from what I can tell, he choked you at the boat ramp and threw you in the lake. Maybe he figured your body would float around and be found so he pulled you out and covered you up. He was leaving as I got there, so he was probably going to get something to dig you a hole."

"Listen, man," he said, rubbing his eyes. "I think I should just go home, okay? Thanks for looking after me."

"Wait," I said, standing. My heart was beating out of my chest. How could he not believe me? "I'll get you some dry clothes. Just please-PLEASE stay right there." He nodded and I took the stairs two at a time up to the yard. Mom and dad had locked me out, which was stupid since I had the van keys. I crept down the hallway to my room. I got Danny some clothes that would be way too big and way too short to fit him and grabbed a hand mirror from the bathroom.

"What're you doing?" my brother asked me from his doorway, nearly making me jump out of my skin.

"Shut up," I said as quietly as I could, sneaking back down the hallway.

"I'll wake 'em up," he said matter-of-factly, not trying to whisper at all.

"I will literally murder you," I said. The look in my eye must have been sufficient, because he called me a slur and shut his door quietly.

Back in the cellar I gave Danny the clothes. His midriff stuck out from the t-shirt and he had to hold the shorts up on his hips. "What's that for?" he asked, pointing to the mirror. I told him to take a deep breath. To not be alarmed. I held the mirror up so he could see his throat. It hurt to see his face as the realization came over him. "He tried to kill me," he said, sitting back down on the table.

"He did kill you," I said. "We've got to call the police."

"Humphrey, don't," he said. He reached out and held my hand. "If we do that, his life will be over. He's the preacher's son." My brain seemed to misfire as he locked his pleading eyes on mine.

"His life should be over," I said, squeezing his hand tightly.

"But so will mine," he whispered. "My dad-hell, my mom. If they know I go to the boat ramp to hook up, especially with guys. They'll never let me out of the house again. I'm probably going to be grounded for the rest of my life as it is."

"They don't have to know any of that," I said. "He needs to be locked up. He picks on you at school all the time. They'll believe it was all premeditated-"

"I'm sorry," Danny said, standing. He pulled his hand free from mine. "I should have been more careful." I sighed and rolled my eyes. I wasn't looking for an apology. I was looking for justice. "We have to let it go," he said. He pulled me in close and squeezed me with all his might. "You saved my life," he said.

"I know you'd do the same," I whispered. But I didn't really believe it. Danny could barely defy his parents' rules, let alone the laws of nature. I deflated in his arms, wanting to just go to sleep.

"No more boat ramp," he said, pulling back. "No more Judd. Let's graduate and get the hell out of here."

The sun was beginning to spill over the horizon when we climbed up out of the cellar. I closed the doors and we stood in the frigid morning, dew settled and sparkling on everything. We decided he should stay with me. They'd believe I went to save him from getting in a car with a drunk friend. They knew I was never invited to parties. Our parents would skin us alive, but at least it was only figurative.

"I feel like I could sleep forever," he said as we crawled in my bed. "Big spoon or little spoon?" he asked. I told him I'd be big. We nestled into each other and I wrapped my arm around him tightly. "Happy Halloween," he said with a sleepy smirk. As he drifted off to sleep, I was still wide awake, making sure I could feel his heartbeat. Making sure he was still breathing. His hair still smelled of rotting things floating in murky water.

The next morning we woke up to a kitchen full of parents. They dourly stared us down as we emerged out of the hallway. "Jesus Christ," Danny's dad exclaimed, seeing the bruises on his neck. He got up and lifted Danny's chin up high to inspect them. Danny winced and clenched his jaw.

"Drinking! Fighting!" Danny's mother said, trying very hard not to shout in someone else's home.

"You should see the other guy," Danny said with a grin. I could see his dad put on the exact same smirk, a tinge of pride in his eyes. For once, I hoped something close to "boys will be boys" would be applied. It seemed like his dad might say it, but looked to his wife.

"That's not funny," Danny's mom said. His dad agreed out loud. "Humphrey, thank you for going to get him last night," she said to me, kindly. It would likely be the last kind thing I heard for a while. They both thanked my parents for raising such a good boy who was such a good friend.

"But we've all decided," my mom said, looking to my dad for support, "you two should spend some time apart. College is coming up quick and you two need to be thinking of your futures."

"Busted," my brother said from the hallway. My mom told him that was incredibly unhelpful.

When they left, my parents laid into me. I didn't care, though. Not really. Danny was alive. There were no apparent side effects to the, all I could think to call it was, resurrection. My first punishment was to wash the van and detail the inside, since I covered it in mud and gravel dust. And of course I'd lose my phone. Any access to the computer (they forgot they had already taken it away from me when I first came out). Maybe I'd get it all back for Christmas. They threatened to make church mandatory, but I told them I'd make a scene. Three times was plenty enough to hear a whole building full of people agree that you deserved to die and burn in hell. Dad threatened to beat me black and blue, but I didn't take it seriously.

Cleaning the van, I realized Danny's hoodie - and his phone - were still inside. Once I had finished the menial labor, I put all of his clothes in the wash. I laid in bed, spinning it around in my hand for a while. There might be something I could use to get Judd in trouble. It would mean invading Danny's privacy, but wasn't that kind of okay? The government could look through anyone's stuff if they thought they might be terrorists. And Judd was definitely something akin.

I finally gave in and flicked the phone open. The battery was nearly depleted. I'd have to be fast. I immediately went to the messages and found "J"'s. I had to believe whatever had happened was a crime of passion. He didn't think to delete anything from

Danny's phone, or throw it in the lake. Maybe he was saving that for the burial.

The most recent messages cleared up a few things. Danny had set out walking in the direction of the boat ramp and Judd had picked him up off the side of the road. It seemed to be a well-practiced routine. I worked my way backward. I saw the dick pics they sent each other. What they were planning on doing to one another. I kept expecting to find the beginning of the messages, but this had been going on for weeks. Why didn't Danny tell me? I knew he'd go out there sometimes, but I didn't know it was always with Judd, of all people. It made me sick. Surely Danny trusted me more than this. More than lying to my face.

If I'm honest with myself, and I think I can do that now all these years later, what bothered me most was the intimacy. Not the sexual stuff. Who cares? I mean the way they spoke to each other. I did eventually find the beginning, and it was very matter of fact. A fly by night tryst out in the dark. But their messages had evolved over time. Eventually they talked about things other than sex. Judd hated his family, which irked me to think we might relate with one another on any level. It seemed like Judd was wanting more than something purely physical. It may have been how well I knew Danny and he didn't, but I could tell Danny didn't feel the same way. Judd was talking about how to make it work, asking Danny to stick around in town instead of going away for college. Judd was going to follow in his dad's footsteps. How pitiful, I thought. Get up and spout hate with the same mouth he used to-

The phone died and I saw my face reflected in its black screen. I looked insane. I likely was insane. I needed to sleep. The phone's body creaked in protest as my fist squeezed around it. This was far from over.

I woke up a few hours later when my mom nudged me awake. "Are these Danny's?" she asked me, holding a pile of dry, folded clothes that smelled of spring breeze or whatever asinine thing they labeled it as. I told her they were. She considered something for a moment, then turned back and slowly shut my door. Something needed to be kept secret from my dad and brother. We had these kinds of chats often, but they were usually fun. When she bought us scratch-offs to do together or a CD that dad would have called "devil music."

35

She sat down on the end of the bed and sighed. She put the clothes on the bed. "You are a good friend, you know that?" she asked. I didn't know what to say, so I didn't say anything. "This isn't easy for me to talk about," she began and my skeleton had the urge to jump out of my skin. "But are you two…" she couldn't even bear to say it.

"No, momma," I said. "We love each other. But not like that."

"But you're both-" she said, looking at my wall of posters. I wanted to make her say the word, but decided to show mercy. I wanted the conversation to be over just as much as she did.

"Yes. But his parents don't know about him," I said. "Please don't tell them." This seemed to hurt her, but I wasn't sure why. She was crying.

"Is that why he got in the fight? Someone being mean to him?" she asked, sniffling.

"I'm not sure," I said. "But I think so. One of the popular boys at school." It wouldn't hurt to plant the seed, in case I could use her in my plot against Judd.

"Baby," she said, laying a heavy hand on my shoulder. "My baby boy. I'm so scared for you. And for him. I think about that boy out in Wyoming. What his momma must have gone through." I knew who she meant. I had spent my high school career checking over my shoulder to be sure it didn't happen to me. I clenched my fists, thinking of how no matter how careful we were, it still happened to Danny.

"We look out for each other," I said. She pulled me into a tight hug and rubbed my back.

"You know I love you," she said, her body shaking with how tightly she held me.

"I do," I said, staring down at my bed. I did know it, but I had so many other more pressing matters on my mind. I pulled away and she reluctantly did the same.

"Take these over to him. But come right back," she said, collecting herself before getting up to leave.

I did what she asked. I knocked on the door and he answered. "Oh hey," he said, clearly happy to see me. The bruises had lightened slightly, but still looked atrocious. "I was just coming to give you your clothes back," he said. We swapped piles, having the right clothes but the smell of one another. "Thanks again," he whispered, clearly guilty. Awkward.

"Don't sweat it," I said. I dug his dead phone out of my pocket and added it to the top of the pile. "That was in your hoodie. I got it out before I did the laundry," I said and he practically collapsed in relief. "They were so mad I lost my phone," he said and we shared a conspiratorial smile. We said we'd see each other at school.

It was very nearly our final week before Christmas Break when people started to notice. Not the bruises, Danny had pulled off a scarf and high-buttoned collars long enough for them to fade by that point. I had spent every day of those few weeks staring Judd down with nothing but hate. He wouldn't even look at Danny. We mostly flew under the radar, keeping to ourselves, but eventually the stray glances turned into calculating examinations.

They noticed how much skinnier Danny had gotten. Already lean and lanky, the loss of much weight at all made him look emaciated. I noticed it long before anyone else did, of course, but he seemed to be okay. When I asked him if he was eating he said, "Yeah, but nothing tastes good. Mom made meatloaf the other night and that was alright, but fruit, vegetables, it's all gross and sour."

Some passages from the old journal came to mind and caused my stomach to fall. H.W.'s specimens had shown violent tendencies and a proclivity for, well I can't say it without sounding like a B monster movie, but "cannibal things". I had no idea if my mixture would have the same effect. Mine had differed so much from H.W.'s in the end. Ingested and not intravenous. I had refused to make any more, however. The bees would simply have to figure out their own collapse without my expert, teenage aid.

"You think he's sick?" I heard Stacy Ingram ask someone in the hallway as we passed. "No, not like the flu. Like AIDS," she said in a terrible approximation of a whisper. I stopped and wheeled around on her. "What, freak?" she asked me, her lip drawn up in disgust.

By the time we had last period, the school was on fire with one last cruel rumor. Everyone had gay uncles their parents had warned them about, who died alone in hospitals in cities far away. "We all took Sex Ed. That's what you get for taking it up the butt," a guy said matter-of-factly with a shrug, watching us. The end of the year had all the teachers and students not even attempting any kind of structure. This allowed even more talk. Even more health text book entries on HIV and AIDS read aloud, like campfire tales.

"I bet West gave it to him," Judd said from behind us. I turned on him. I took my glasses off so he could see my eyes. See that I knew what he had done. See that this was all his fault.

"Yeah right, West is a virgin," Emily said, which got some really great laughs.

"That bitch," I muttered to Danny.

Danny didn't let it bother him. But that worried me too. His eyes were glassy. He didn't seem bothered by anything. It seemed in order to get through to him I had to wade out into the sea of indifference that was coming up over his ears.

"You don't have to have sex to pass it," someone offered to the conversation. "You can get it by touching them. Or if they get their blood on you."

As much as I hate to say it, this gave me an idea.

I invited Danny to my house for scary movies. Danny was my responsibility. I had to do something.

The DVD menu for our chosen zombie flick was on loop. The grainy black and white snippets featured a horde of the stumbling, jerking corpses. Hunger made manifest, they crawled out of mausoleums and mealy graves. A warbly theremin accompanied a violin that squealed along with the sex-crazed coeds who were going to get devoured. Danny sat, bathed in the TV's glow. His eyes were half-closed in a way that reminded me of the night he died. In the blink of an eye, I saw him covered in leaf litter, lake water dripping down his nose.

Trying to wipe the image away, I brought my face close to Danny's. "They're coming to get you, Danny," I said, chomping at him. He gave me a pity laugh and gently pushed me away. I got up and asked if he wanted a milkshake. He said no, that he didn't have an appetite. And besides, it was freezing outside. I went to the kitchen and made enough for both of us anyway. This was my next experiment and I hoped it would work. Perhaps hot cocoa would have been a better idea, but I was worried the heat might neutralize my secret ingredient.

The gnashing blades of the blender drowned out everything and I watched the ice cream be pulverized. Looking this way and that to make sure no one was looking, I took a knife from the block by the sink. Selecting the smallest one with a sharp tip, I hesitated. Now's not the time to wuss out, Humphrey. Danny needs you, I thought.

It took more effort than I thought it would to dig the blade into the tip of my finger. Once it punched through my skin, however, the tip went deep into the flesh. "Fuck," I muttered as my body caught up to the trauma, the incision burning and my pulse pumping. I held my dripping finger over the blender and was surprised at how quickly the red splashes vanished, blended into obscurity. I wasn't sure how much to put in, but I didn't want anyone to catch me, so I shook a few more droplets free and wrapped my finger in a paper towel. I poured the mixture into two glasses and thoroughly washed the blender. I immediately regretted using my pointer finger for the procedure, but science is founded on trial and error. Two fast food straws from the junk drawer completed the presentation.

I stared at the glasses, sitting there as if they weren't anything but ordinary milkshakes. Clenching my finger tightly to try and get it to stop bleeding, I had the briefest moment of doubt. If I was wrong, what I was doing was at the very least a tiny bit insane. Not certifiable lock me away insane, though. Just kooky. Certainly not "touched" as my mom called her sister who went to the state hospital and didn't come back. I thought of her there, looking out through the crawling ivy. I clamped my eyes shut and forced my mind to stop running away with every errant thought. I told myself to consider the what if of being right. If I was right…would that make it any less insane? My glasses had slipped down to nearly falling off my nose by the time I came back to reality. I poked my head back into the living room and got nervous, thinking Danny had already fallen asleep. Insane or not, this hypothesis needed testing.

I went back to the couch and handed Danny his glass. He said he didn't want it. I insisted. "Okay, if it will appease you," he said in faux exasperation that I was pretty sure wasn't fake at all. He took a tiny pull and smacked his lips. "Delicious, thank you," he said absentmindedly, handing me back the glass. Damn, a failure after all, I thought. I made to take the glass back but he pulled it back to his mouth. He greedily sucked on the straw. A wave of relief passed over me as I saw more light in his eyes than I had in a month. "What did you put in this, crack?" he asked as he abandoned the straw and took heaving gulps of the milkshake. It flooded his mouth and dribbled down the sides of his chin.

"I thought you might like it," I said, self-satisfied. He finished his and barely stopping to catch his breath, asked if I was going to finish mine. I hadn't even taken a sip, but I wasn't too keen on drinking my own blood anyway. I handed it over to him and in a few moments it was gone. Danny leaned back in the cushions and took heavy breaths, patting his stomach, which was slightly bulging against his t-shirt. He noticed my finger and pulled the paper towel away. The little gash oozed slightly, my blood shining in the dark. "How did you cut yourself making milkshakes?" he asked and his crooked grin and sleepy laugh made my heart soar.

We never got around to watching the movie. Danny leaned over and placed his head in my lap. I played with his hair, which was soft and smelled like sweat. "I've felt so strange lately," he said to the TV. Despite what he had said, he sounded content. When I asked him what he meant, he didn't answer. He was fast asleep. I wasn't sure how I was going to keep feeding him in this meaningful way, but that was a problem for another night. That night, I was happy to have my friend.

It's not uncommon to cut yourself in the kitchen. It is, however, uncommon to manage a cut on each and every finger. I did my best to avoid looking like Seymour in The Little Shop of Horrors, hands mummified in band-aids. Instead, I had managed a system of blood-letting from places no one would see, especially in the winter. I asked my mom to make more red meat. She said I was getting pale, that maybe I needed to be checked for anemia.

Danny, on the other hand, flourished. The color had returned to his cheeks and the rumors of him having AIDS went away. He was no Audrey II, however.

He had no idea what I had been doing. We shared at least five meals a week together at school, and some in the evening or on the weekends if we were hanging out, which we usually were. When he wasn't looking or got up to use the bathroom, I'd drop a little or a lot of blood from one of my vials into whatever he was eating or drinking.

Danny noticed, sometimes. I found soda to be the most effective vehicle. If he off-handedly mentioned a metallic taste, I'd point out that he was drinking from a metal can. His appetite for normal food had been re-established. It seemed the longer I fed him my blood, the more his senses heightened. He'd point out conversations people were having across the lunch room, or notice colors he had a hard time describing. More than a few times, it seemed he read my mind. When I was quiet, thinking about the future or how I was going to get Judd arrested, he would ask what I was thinking about. His eyes would dance between mine and I could tell he knew the answer. I lied, anyway.

I kept track of my observations in the H.W. journal. I really should have given it up, but I wanted to make sure I had data to form the idea of trends.

Without any blood, it took him about a week to get gaunt. I only let it happen the once, when we were on Christmas break and I didn't have any choice. He came back from his grandparents looking worse for wear. He usually did, as they took every opportunity to remind him he should be looking for a pretty girl to marry and get pregnant. But there was a deeper agitation, something more akin to a tiger pacing its cage.

I got the inkling to test more than just blood. Not a serious plan, you understand. But when my brother was especially cruel on Christmas morning I wondered if I let Danny get hungry enough if he would take care of the problem for me. My house was littered with murder tools, used to carve up deer and erase coyotes from the face of the earth. But no, I would think, I wouldn't want to put Danny in that situation. He was kind and smart. I was wretched and ugly, and I never wanted him to be those things.

On New Year's, we watched the ball drop by ourselves. Our parents were at a party and my brother was getting high with his friends. We got a man outside the gas station to buy us 40s. We had taped them to our hands, Edward 40hands it was called. By midnight the beer that was left in the bottles was hot from our hands. We clinked all four of our bottles and shared a little kiss. Then burst into laughter. We watched the people milling around Times Square for a little while. "Humphrey," Danny said, his head laid against the couch, watching me closely.

"Yes?" I asked, draining the sudsy dregs of one of my bottles.

"I love you," he said. "I just wanted you to know that."

"I love you too," I said without much consideration. I started to bite at the tape around my hand to free the empty bottle.

"Hey," he said, kicking my leg. I turned to give him my full, albeit drunk, attention. "I mean it."

"I mean it, too," I said. He seemed to be searching, maybe trying to read my mind again.

"I keep thinking about that night," he said, sadly. "No matter how hard I try, I can't remember anything before I woke up here, with you." It was my turn to try and read his mind. Was he going to confront me about the blood? Was he ready to try and incriminate Judd? My beer-addled brain stumbled down that path quickly.

It had been months. There was no physical evidence to speak of. Maybe we could search on the internet for the statute of limitations for assault. "I just wanted to say thank you, again," he said. My mind hit a brick wall. I told him not to mention it, then sulked as I sucked on the other bottle. "We have to start applying to Miskatonic soon," he said.

"Please, not tonight," I said, agitated.

"It's the new year," he said with an arched eyebrow. "Just a few months and we'll walk the line. Then we'll get out of this shit hole."

"I'm not sure I even want to go," I said. But if he was going, I would need to as well. If he wasted away to nothing it would be my fault. If he got so hungry he lost control, I'd never forgive myself. The stilted rock tumbler of my mind spun again. Maybe it would be best to tell him. He might be mad, but we were best friends. Best friends didn't stay mad at each other forever. I looked at him, about to speak, and he looked back expectantly.

I saw the van's headlights bob and jerk into the driveway. "Shit," I said, stumbling to get away. I turned the TV and all the lights off and we made a mad dash for my room. "Help me!" I whisper-yelled and we could hardly breathe we were laughing so loud. Between giggles we tugged and tore at the tape. I shoved all the bottles into one of my drawers and we jumped into bed. We assumed "natural" sleeping positions just as my door creaked open.

"They should be out having a good time," my dad said, and it was maybe the most good-natured thing he had ever said about me.

"They're good boys," my mom said, clearly drunk. They continued to talk as she shut the door. Danny and I buried our heads under the covers and tried to suppress our laughing fit. The air under the blanket was hot so I emerged and pulled off my shirt, throwing it on the floor. Danny did the same. We breathed deeply, looking at each other from across the pillows. Danny reached out and traced a finger down my arm. He stopped at the row of scabs near my armpit.

"What's this?" Danny asked. I could hear the fear and concern in his voice.

"Nothing," I said, turning over, tugging the blanket up. I felt his chin on my shoulder and his breath on my ear.

"You would tell me, right?" he asked. "If you needed help?"

"I would, yeah," I said. "But I don't." He was the one who needed help. And I was giving it to him. That's what friends are for, I thought to myself. The room felt big and empty as the silence stretched between us. I thought he may have fallen asleep, but he moved again, throwing his arm over me and hugging me close.

"Do you promise?" he asked and I could tell he was fighting sleep.

"Cross my heart," I said, but before I could add "Hope to die", he shushed me and squeezed me tightly.

"No dying," Danny said. I thought of his pale blue skin and the terrible tint of the bruises on his neck.

"No dying," I agreed.

I'm not sure what time it was when I awoke to find Danny standing at the side of my bed. I was laying on my back. In a half-dream state I opened my eyes and saw his silhouette. It had started to snow while we, at least I, slept. Danny's breath was ragged and slow. His pupils glowed like that of a cat or a dog in the night. He blinked and the shine remained. I looked down and realized one of my cuts had come open in the night.

"I don't feel so good," Danny whispered. His shoulders raised and fell. The light coming through the blinds filled the pool of his sunken chest. I stood slowly and looked up into his face. "I don't know if you should do that," he said. I touched my finger to the scab and felt the warm blood spill out onto my finger.

"It's okay," I said. I offered him the tip of my finger. He put the back of his hand to his mouth. But he didn't move away. I took his arm in my other hand and gently lowered it.

"What's happening?" he asked as he bowed his head. He took the tip of my finger into his mouth and licked it clean.

"You're hungry, that's all."

Danny didn't talk to me until we went back to school after Winter Break. Even then it wasn't until our final class of the day. We sat together at lunch, as always, but he just stared at his pizza and picked it into little pieces. Danny peeled the government cheese away, revealing the red underneath. He let me talk to him, but he wouldn't say anything back. "Library after school," he wrote in his notebook and turned it to me. I couldn't hide the enormous sigh of relief that escaped me.

Once we were within the hallowed, holy halls of the library, I nudged him. I thought it was playful, but he turned and looked like he might punch me. I threw my hands up. "What's crawled up your ass?" I asked, throwing my book bag onto a nearby table.

"Are you serious?" he asked. He slung his own backpack around and dumped out a pile of books. They were a mixture of library titles. Guides to vampires in mythology. Zombie lore through the ages. Behind the scenes of the Universal Dracula with Bela Lugosi. I looked between him and the books.

"Okay?" I asked. I wondered what I was missing. "Are you wanting to write fan fiction or something?"

Danny gripped a nearby chair so hard his knuckles turned white. I heard the wood whine against his hands. "You're not funny," he said seriously. I lied and said I wasn't trying to be. "Now that I know what it is," he whispered, "I want it all the time." He looked so scared it broke my heart. This is why I didn't want him to know. But we had crossed and burned that bridge simultaneously.

"You can just ask," I said, rolling up my sleeve. His hand shot out and grabbed my upper arm. His fingers dug into my skin through my shirt. I felt one of the scabs break loose and ooze. "You're hurting me," I said calmly. No need to start something. I had faith he didn't realize what he was doing. He let go and I could see the instant remorse wash over him.

"Did I..." he said, trying to rack his brain. "Am I...?" His cheeks blossomed with blush.

"Are you...a vampire? A zombie?" I asked, incredulous. I picked up one of the books and flipped through it. There was an illustration of a young man, eyes crazed, half naked, being held at arm's length by his victim. I caught myself drawing comparisons, but tried to play it off. The blush deepened and he watched the table. "You're so dramatic," I said, snapping the book shut. "Did you plan all...this?" I asked, gesturing to the pile of books and his defensive stance. I really did mean it as a friendly dig, to make him laugh and stop being so nervous.

"Fuck off," he said, grabbing his backpack and heading for the door.

"Danny, wait!" I called after him, trying to get my things together. Danny smashed into the door and it flung back, breaking the piston that pulled it shut. He didn't stop and stomped out into the parking lot. Didn't even think of looking back.

The librarian came out of her lair, yowling like a wet cat. I told her one of the football players did it. I couldn't remember his name, I told her, but I was pretty sure it was the main one. The captain or whatever they called it.

I collected the pile of books and took them home. Spreading them out on my bed, I realized one of them was his notebook. I thumbed through it, seeing a flipbook of our conversations, some story ideas we brainstormed, us making plans.

I paused momentarily on a sketch he had done in pen. It was of me, at my desk, titled "The Test". He must have done it after a quiz he had breezed through then watched me suffer and stumble through the rest of the allotted time. One hand was gripping my hair while the other marked a bubble. My glasses seemed to barely hang on to the tip of my nose, looking like they might fall off at any second. The proportions were a little off, but it really wasn't bad. I kept flipping.

The last filled in page was a collection of notes from the books. Of course he treated this like any other homework. And of course he'd get library books, when there were perfectly good sources online.

He had compiled a list of his symptoms: poor sleep, nightmares (of what, I wondered), heightened senses, and lastly, rather ominously, the word "cravings". His normal handwriting was slower here, more methodical, as if he had trouble writing it. I had pieced together the last two items in my own observations, but I didn't know he hadn't been sleeping. My assumption was he was too hungry to sleep sometimes. And the nightmares were likely related to his murder. But I couldn't find any evidence to that point.

Below this list he had written out two columns of facts, one about zombies, and one about vampires. Of course there were dozens of iterations for either, all of which we'd watched in movies late at night. Strigoi and Boo Hags. What worried me, however, was in the zombie column. I found the appropriate book and read alongside. There was a chapter on Haitian zombies created by witches, who "resurrected" people they had poisoned into a false death. These victims would become mindless servants enthralled to said witch.

In Danny's notes, among the cramped scribbles, stood "Mind control" and to the side "Humphrey?"

Things were a little strained between us for a few days. But as I said, best friends don't stay mad at each other for long. I returned the library books and his notebook, which I didn't mention and neither did he. I stopped giving him my blood and instead gave him time to consider.

One day he trudged across his yard, into mine, and asked if he could talk to me. He looked drawn again already, which concerned me. He had become accustomed to a steady supply. Either that or the longer it went on, the greater the hunger became. I didn't see that as a worthwhile conclusion to jump to, though.

Back in the cellar, where it all began, I could tell he was struggling to find the words. He was ashamed. I didn't understand that. I didn't take much care in how I held my head or followed him with my eyes as he paced the dank depths of the room. "Stop looking at me like that," he finally said, throwing his arms in the air.

"Like what?" I asked coolly.

"Like I'm one of your experiments!" he said. He was gripping his stomach.

"You're not one of my experiments," I lied. It's not as though I thought of him as only a specimen. I never lied when I said I loved him. But he was, in fact, my greatest experiment. He let out a yell and punched one of the support beams. It creaked and splintered where his knuckles made contact. I tried not to immediately quantify the reaction, but I did make a mental note to jot it down later. "Here," I said, going to the mini fridge. I pulled out one of the vials of blood and tossed it to him.

"This is sick!" he shouted, but he didn't let go of the blood.

"How so?" I asked. I sat down and pushed my glasses up my nose. "You have the need to consume blood. Maybe flesh, too. I don't know for certain. But it's a biological need. Like breathing or sleeping. There's no moral weight to it."

"It's not normal," he said feebly as he swirled the dark red liquid and watched it slide down the sides.

"Normal? Since when do you care about normal?" I asked. His eyes were glued to the blood. I kept waiting for him to drink it, but he was still reluctant. "Oh for fuck's sake," I said, standing up and yanking the vial away from him. I unscrewed the cap and gave it back to him. "Do you want me to turn away? Will that make you feel better?" We stood and stared at each other for a moment.

"Actually…yeah," he said, looking at the ground. I said I was happy to oblige. I turned away and heard him gulp down what was there. I hazarded a look behind me and saw he was licking the inside clean, his eyes closed in rapture. I was looking away again by the time he told me I could turn around. "I need to go to the doctor," he said with a little burp.

"I'll take you, if you want," I said. "I don't advise it. I'm not sure how they'd react. Probably put you away."

"Don't do that," he said. "Don't just try to scare me."

"I'm being serious," I said. "You can tell them everything. I'll probably be put away, too. But I won't stop you. If you think they can take better care of you than I can, we'll go right now."

"Humphrey, you're being a real dick right now," he said. I couldn't help but smirk. He looked like he wanted to punch me square in the face. Judging by what he'd done to the beam, I'm glad he didn't. "What did you do to me?"

"If you're ready to actually accept the truth," I said, feeling petty, "you died that night. Judd killed you. I brought you back. Just like I told you." I took a deep breath and sighed. "But I'll admit, I really didn't know what the fuck I was doing. Still don't know. My serum worked and you came back. We're clearly just dealing with the side effects."

"Side effects? You could have poisoned me!" he said.

"As I said, you were already dead." He fixed a wilting glare on me. "You and a single bee are my only confirmed subjects. I haven't made any more of the solution since then," I said.

"Why not? Don't you want to save the bees?" he asked, properly derailed from his frustration. "You wouldn't shut up about the damn bees." He stood at the bottom of the cellar stairs and stared up into the sun. "You could sell the formula, you'd be rich. Humphrey West, the boy who cured death." My predecessor's work had been halted abruptly, I didn't take this as a coincidence. No matter how his notes called to me at night, I needed to keep them shut and shrouded in darkness.

"I saved you. That's enough for me," I said. "However happy I am to have you back, I'm not sure the potion going into mass production would be great for the world. And who knows if I could even recreate it reliably. It's entirely possible we hit the exact right circumstances to reanimate a human body and to do so again would be like winning several lotteries at once. It was Halloween night. A full moon. Who's to say what could have affected the outcome." I realized I had been rambling and I wasn't sure if any of it had gotten through. He turned his hand in the sunlight, inspecting it. I couldn't be sure what for. Maybe signs of rot? Nosferatu claws? I came up behind him and wrapped my arms around his waist. My head only hit between his shoulder blades. "Magic or miracle. Whatever it was, you're back."

"I guess you're right," he mumbled. He turned and gingerly broke free of my embrace. He walked to a row of jars and dragged his finger along their dusty tops. "You forgot the part where it turned me into some kind of monster," he said to the pickled vegetables in their murky baths. I had intentionally left out any mention of that particular side effect, but it had certainly crossed my mind. I couldn't be responsible for more than one…whatever term might apply to him.

"No more of that," I said, waving away the words that crowded the air. "I will happily give you whatever you need. Admittedly, we don't have a failsafe if something should happen to me. But now I don't have to keep anything a secret from you. We can start ironing out all those details."

"Why did you keep it a secret, Humphrey?" he asked. I could only think of snarky things to say about him not believing me when I did try to tell him. So instead I kept my mouth shut. After a beat he clutched the hair above his forehead in frustration. "This is insane," he said, exasperated. His shoulders slumped and he looked like he might weigh roughly a million pounds.

"We'll go to Miskatonic," I said resolutely. "I'll go the medical track and develop a cure. Who knows, maybe by then you won't even need your," I said and twirled my hand dismissively, "special diet." I went to the refrigerator and pulled out a few more vials I had stockpiled. "Here, so you have them. Keep them somewhere cold and safe." Danny's eyes flitted between the vials and my face. I did my best to smile. Nothing strange here. A friend giving a gift he made himself. Danny's tongue rolled along his bottom lip as he considered. He took the blood and put it in his coat pocket, turning away brusquely. "I love you, Danny," I said to his back. His hands balled into fists and his head hung low. If he said something, I didn't hear it. He trudged up the steps and out into the bleak winter sunlight.

"I don't trust it," my dad said, turning the jar of honey this way and that in the light of the kitchen. The typical amber hue of honey had been supplanted by a bright green tinge. It was spring now, and the McCoy's bees hadn't succumbed to Colony Collapse Disorder. The McCoy's had dropped off a sample of the bees' latest bounty. They were taking it to the university to get tested, but wanted my dad's "expert" opinion, too. I rabidly chewed at the flesh by my thumbnail. Could the bees have propagated my concoction? Was there a hive, hives even, of bees that were literally out for blood? Undying and unceasingly productive?

"The bees probably just got into something. It tastes just fine," my mom said. My stomach lurched. If the honey did contain a form of my creation, what effect would it have on a living person? I kept close tabs on my mom for the next little bit, but didn't notice anything out of the ordinary.

When I told Danny about it, he shrugged. "Do you want to go to prom with me?" he asked. I had a hard time making the mental leap across the gap in topics. I couldn't be positive, but I was almost certain we would be the first gay guys, maybe in the whole state, to go to prom together. I could already hear the whispers, see the sideways glances.

"I would be honored," I said. "But if either of us wins Prom King or Queen, we have to make a pact to run for it. There's no way I'm letting you or me get Carrie'd".

"It may not be so bad to be covered in blood," he said, doodling in his notebook. I looked around to make sure no one had heard him. "Do you happen to have any more with you?" he asked. His fist closed around his shirt at his stomach.

"I gave you what I had at lunch," I said. "But I can go to the bathroom and get you more," I added quickly. Danny handed me the vials I had given him just that morning, spotless and clean.

"Fuck," Judd said from somewhere else in the room. I turned to see bright blood droplets dotting his textbook. Another fell to the page with a pang and I felt Danny go rigid beside me. The teacher excused Judd and as he walked out, Danny was laser-focused, keeping his body entirely still as his eyes swiveled. I volunteered to go help. This got a confused murmur from around the room, but the teacher gave me a dismissive wave of her hand.

In the boy's bathroom, which reeked of piss and marginal attempts at sanitation, I caught up to Judd. He was at the mirror, tilting his head back.

"Don't do that," I said. "You'll just swallow the blood and it will make you nauseous."

"I didn't ask for your input, queerbait," he said, his voice muffled and congested.

"Here," I said, taking the paper towel from him. He grabbed hold of my collar and held it, glaring at me. Blood dripped down onto his lip. My heart was racing. I had never been this close to Judd in my life. It occurred to me that I could hurt him. Probably not very effectively, being a full foot shorter. But I could really make him bleed, I bet. There were sharp corners and rusty screws all over the place. I yanked my arm free and pointed to the sink. "Lean over it and pinch the bridge of your nose, here." I touched the spot and he winced. Surprisingly, he followed my direction. I eyed the blood that was beginning to settle at the bottom of the sink. "Why did you do it?" I asked.

"Get a nose bleed? That's not my fault, bro," he said, offended.

"I mean kill Danny," I said. He did the typical blustering and denying. He had no idea what I was talking about. Danny obviously wasn't dead.

"What the fuck is wrong with you?" he asked. But I saw in his eyes he was scared. And I won't deny it, that fact excited me. I held some power over Judd Thomas. A statistical impossibility.

"I know what you did. And one day you'll pay for it," I said. Judd suckerpunched me, right in the stomach. All the air rushed out of me and I couldn't get any of it back. He shoved me so hard I flew back into the wall, slamming my head against the paper towel dispenser. "Good...idea," I said, not wanting to give him the satisfaction of seeing me struggle. "Kill me...at school."

"Stay away from me, freak," he said and hocked a bloody loogie at my feet. He left the bathroom in a huff. I groaned and leaned forward. I touched the crown of my head and my fingers came away covered in blood. Saved me some trouble, I thought. I harvested what blood I could and put it in one of the vials. I squeezed a drop or two from Judd's paper towel and collected a little bit more from the sink and added it to my own. Admittedly, I was curious what effect this might have.

Getting back to class, I sat down next to Danny and passed him the vial.

"What did you do?" Danny asked, leaning close. Judd was back in his seat, and I could tell he was talking about me by the way everyone's eyes kept darting in my direction.

"That's disgusting," Emily said loudly. "I can't believe Humphrey would corner you in the bathroom like that. You should tell the counselor."

"I'm not scared of him," he said in response, but was looking directly at me. I looked back and grinned.

All I could think was, "you should be."

Danny also got permission to go to the bathroom, the teacher saying her patience was wearing thin. When he came back he seemed calmer, warmer. He passed me the empty vial. "Did you change something?" he wrote in my notebook.

"Why?" I replied.

"It tasted different," he scribbled. "Better? A kind of gym sock undertaste." A mean, sickly green stripe of jealousy ran up my spine. Better? Did I taste bad? What exactly was my "undertaste"? While I thought of what to say in reply, I heard him sniffing. He leaned in close, smelling my hair. I leaned back and gently pushed him away. No one seemed to notice. His pupils were enormous. His ribs pushed against his shirt as he breathed like he had New Year's Eve.

I distracted him with preparations for prom. Eventually we settled into a heated debate on what colors to wear. He wanted a white tux, which I told him was foolish at best. I wanted a green tie and he wanted a red one. I told him it was prom, not Christmas. He playfully grabbed my arm to keep me from writing more and we froze like that. Danny squeezed his hand tighter and I felt the blood flow constrict. My pulse pounded against his hand and it grew tighter. I pulled our arms below the desk and wrenched him free. "I'll give you more ASAP," I wrote.

His handwriting was tremulous as he wrote, "Good."

We prepared for prom at my house. Changing into our rented suits, I looked over his body. My fears had been confirmed over the weeks leading up to that night. My blood was resulting in diminishing returns. Maybe it was how I ate. Or maybe a wider variety was needed to provide adequate nutrients. I felt like a rung-out wash rag, but it wasn't enough. I could tell his body was, perhaps not decaying, but certainly getting worn down. His legs seemed considerably less hairy. The slight bit of chest and belly hair he had the previous summer was gone entirely. He didn't pay me any mind as he donned the white button-up. I caught sight of some scratches down the length of his forearms. I did my best to ask what had happened in a nonchalant way. He paused to look at them. "Stupid cat attacked me," he said in a way that asked me to drop it. The Morelands didn't have a cat.

"Did you…" I began and his body rippled into a defensive posture. I cleared my throat nervously. I despised myself for feeling this way, but I had become afraid of Danny. His hunger was getting harder and harder for him to manage. We still did normal teenage stuff. Took our ACTs and applied to college. Went to the movies and killed time at the mall. But there was always a slight undertow of dread. I worried that someone might accidentally hurt themselves and I'd have to pry my blood-yearning friend away. It had yet to happen, but it felt inevitable. I was dreading prom because people do stupid things. Sometimes they break glass and cut themselves. Sometimes they're drunk and sway too hard into a sharp corner. I would have to be on my toes. Starting a fight before we even left my house was not part of the plan, but that curiosity, the morbid fascination I could never deny, took hold. Perhaps I shouldn't mention the cat and its curiosity. "Danny," I said quietly. "Did you…eat a cat? I won't judge you. I just need to know." He looked at me for a minute's eternity, blinking slowly. I imagined if he had fur, his hackles would be raised on end.

"Humbug?" my mom called from outside the door. "Are you decent?" I told her we were, so she came in and started taking pictures. She had originally hated the idea of us going together, the ridicule we might face. But I told her we weren't scared and she shouldn't be either. How foolish we were. In that moment, she was giddy, burning through a disposable camera like it had infinite film.

I was impressed with Danny's real boy mask. He never put up a front with me, or rather I thought he didn't, so it was interesting to see him do so. If you didn't know any better, he was just a 17 year old with jitters over his senior prom. "So handsome!" she said. We fixed Danny's hair, combing it over to the side, which made him look like an old movie star. I didn't even bother with mine. I knew I'd be nervously running my fingers through it all night.

We didn't rent a limo or anything egregious. It was just the two of us. Mom let me take the van (as long as I swore on my grandma's grave I would not drink a single sip of alcohol). We rode to the school in relative silence. I put on some emo rock, some song about vampires that made me nervous about how Danny might react. But Danny just watched the farms and churches fly by the window. "I wasn't accusing you of anything, you know," I said flatly.

"What if I did it?" Danny asked. "Would you consider me a failure? Start from scratch?"

"Danny," I said, scolding. "As long as you didn't leave a note confessing, I couldn't care less. I ask because the more information I have, the better I can care for you."

"Maybe I don't want you caring for me," Danny said. "I'm so sick of you micromanaging everything I do. Like I'm a ticking time bomb!" We drove for a little while in silence while I formulated what to say. I wanted to lay it all out. Be nasty about it. I was giving him my literal blood, sweat and tears. I was weak and hadn't slept a full night in half a year. "I feel like this is exactly what you wanted," he said, and I could tell he was crying. "I'm totally dependent on you and that puts me right where you want me." He let out a frustrated groan. "And look at you now! Just calm and collected. You're physically incapable of having a single human emotion, Humphrey."

"I didn't plan on you getting murdered, asshole," I said raising my voice. If he wanted me to show emotion, I was happy to. "But you had to fuck a straight boy didn't you? And it got you fucking killed." He looked at me and I stared back. "Not to worry though, Humphrey will fix it, right? He'll literally bleed himself dry to make sure I stay alive. Isn't that right? I think you've forgotten who has who where, exactly." My face was red in the rearview mirror as I punched the steering wheel.

We pulled into the school and I parked as far away as I could. We both breathed in little shallow spurts, furious with each other, angry tears falling on our shirts. I looked at the school's side door. Limos of varying ridiculous degrees were dropping off their contents, kids who had eaten Olive Garden and pre-gamed on the ride over. Oh, to be in the peak of my life, not a care in the world. I both pitied and resented them. The vast majority of them would get married and start procreating. They'd get divorced and remarry someone else from our graduating class and start the cycle all over again. Descendants' descendants spread out in a line into the future, not budging an inch from this dogshit town.

"I need you to know," I said calmly, trying to compose myself. "You are free to do whatever you want. Kill and eat pets, people even. You are not beholden to me, or this town, or your family. You can leave right now and if you told me not to follow, I wouldn't. But if you asked me to come, I'd be happy to. Does that qualify as a human emotion?" I asked, still feeling like being a bit of a prick.

"I shouldn't have said that," he said, rubbing his temples and snorting snot back up his nose. "And I'm sorry. Thank you for everything you've-" he began.

"Well good, glad that's settled," I said, unbuckling and turning the car off. "Let's go." I got out and started walking towards the school. Danny caught up to me in only a few long strides. He grabbed hold of my hand and laced his fingers through mine. We were already attracting some attention from not only the students, but some of the chaperones as well.

The principal met us in the parking lot, intercepting our entry. "Sorry, boys, I appreciate your 'statement.' Attempting some activism and all that. But we all know same sex dates are not allowed to school functions."

"Bobby and Sean came together as friends," I said, pointing to them as they got their tickets punched. "Are we not allowed to come as friends?"

"Forget it, Humphrey," Danny said, rolling his eyes and turning away. I didn't move. I adjusted my glasses and squared up, trying to stand as tall as Principal Owens.

"You know we have a Zero Tolerance policy for violence, Mr. West," Owens said in a sing-song way. I felt anger boiling in my stomach.

"We are students here," I said. "We are entering prom as friends. You can ask anybody."

"What's going on, Mr. Owens?" Judd asked, sauntering towards them. I couldn't contain my disgust. Owens clearly appreciated the back up.

"Are you going to make us come in separate from one another? That's pointless," I said.

"I'm afraid you're not welcome at this time," Owens said, having perfected the "it's out of my hands" body language. I felt little flashes in my mind, tiny snippets of the last few months. How many cuts had I endured? How many indignities? All because Judd Thomas panicked and killed my friend. It felt as though all these thoughts were a roiling hive of bees, drowning out the world. I wished one of the limos would mow them both down. I wished a lightning strike would hit Judd and arc off of his tacky gold necklace and fry Owens. I wished bees would descend on them and sting and tear every inch of their bodies. My head filled with frenzied buzzing.

I was briefly stunned out of my anger as a bee darted from a nearby bush and smacked into Judd's face. "What the fuck?" he yelled, followed by "Ow! Shit!" as it stung him. He swatted at it, then stomped it where it landed on the ground. I took a step back as a horrific hum lifted from the spring flowers and the mulch of the school's landscaping. In the blink of an eye, a veritable swarm had coated Owens and Judd both. They ran towards the building, clawing at the little beasts as they buried pulsating stingers into their skin.

"What was that?" Danny asked, amazed.

I stooped down to inspect the bee Judd had stepped on. Its stinger was gone, of course, and it had been mashed into the pavement. But it still wriggled. I swept it up onto my palm. The setting sun reflected green in its eye and it's hard to describe what all I felt. Pride? Wonder? Pity for this tiny thing that sacrificed itself for my defense? "Poor thing," I said, bringing it up to my face. One of its antennae was broken, but the other still danced about. I didn't have long to eulogize its insect soul, because in a flurry of iridescent wings, it flew off, back to its business.

"That's not right," Danny said, looking over my shoulder. "Is it bad I kind of wanted to…" Danny said, trying to find the words. "Kinda sorta rip his face off?"

"Not in my book," I said with a shrug. "Shall we?" I asked, holding my hand out for Danny. He looked at me in disbelief, but in a happy, kind of "you're nuts!" way. His hand fit into mine and we strolled into the prom as if nothing had happened.

"What's going on?" one of Judd's friends asked as we came in. "Judd's face looks like a meat balloon."

"It was weird!" I said, adopting his idiot affectation. "All these bees just came out of nowhere and attacked him!"

"Whoa!" he said and then ran off to tell anyone who would listen. As we walked the relatively empty halls, buzzing bumblebees flew the opposite direction, back to their tiny worlds.

We entered the gym and found the dance floor deserted. Everyone was too busy fawning over Judd and Mr. Owens. The Prom Committee had chosen "Paris Nights" (how pedestrian) as our theme that year. There were plywood eiffel towers and fairy lights strung up everywhere in a tangled web. An inferno waiting to happen. There were words like "bonjour" and "Paris" on sticks for a photo booth. There was a crimson punch and plates of already sliced cake, growing stale and crumbly by the second.

But don't allow my callous musings to paint an ugly picture. It was beautiful. Danny was beautiful. He looked up, as he often did, with wonder. He might have been on the Prom Committee if being my friend hadn't made him a pariah all these years. The DJ was still playing music so we just went out onto the dance floor. There were plenty of sneers and jeers thrown our way. "Wacko", "sick fuck", "freak", "demon", the usual. How could they possibly link me to a bee attack? That was preposterous. I laughed out loud with the idea as we twirled about.

Danny and I danced with a wild abandon. Eventually, there wasn't anything else for the onlookers to do except join. The music slowed down and we took the opportunity to take a break from jerking and throwing our bodies around. I rested my head against Danny's chest and we slowly swayed back and forth. My glasses askew, my ear to his sternum, I heard his heart. It was pumping hard and that made me smile.

When I opened my eyes, I saw Judd staring at me, sprawled out in a chair. All his lunk lackeys were at the table with him, moping in solidarity. He held a weeping bag of ice against his eye, which had swollen shut. His lips were moving and his one open eye had a naked rage dancing in it. The song stopped and we pulled apart. I got on my tip-toes and kissed Danny on the cheek. Judd practically combusted with anger.

"What was that for?" he asked with a sweaty smile.

"Just a little 'sorry' for earlier, that's all," I said and readjusted my glasses. When I looked back at Judd's table, it was empty. I got a nagging feeling, but dismissed it. Let him go home and lick his wounds. Or rather, go to Emily's after party and get piss the bed drunk.

Eventually, people started trickling away to said parties. "What do you think?" Danny asked. "Want to go?"

"Nah, not really," I said, shrugging. We had loosened our ties and were meandering out towards the parking lot. "Unless you do." We passed the dark hallways that seemed to stretch out into nothing. Emergency exit signs glowed red down each one, adding to the eerie air. Distant shouts and squeals reverberated off the walls and I imagined it finally resembled the prison or asylum it often felt like. I turned to look at Danny and saw he was looking at me.

No, not at me, past me, into the darkness. His pupils shone, but his face was contorted in shock. He was reaching for me as I turned to see what he was looking at. Something struck me on the top of my head and the jolt made me bite deeply into my tongue. My whole body seized, electric jolts running down to the tips of my fingers. I felt a warm, trickling flow of blood rush down my forehead and fork around my nose. I fell backward into Danny, who was screaming. Judd stood over me with a baseball bat and he seemed to multiply as two of his cronies, Devon and Liam, appeared out of the black hallway. My eyes rolled back in my head and everything went dark.

I woke to water being splashed on my face. I felt like my skull had split in two and my brain was exposed to the open air. There were bright lights in my face. I tried to shield my eyes but my arms were bound behind me. I looked about and found I was tied to a tree. The lights had blinded me, and I couldn't see out into the darkness around me. "Danny?" I called out. My voice was hoarse and my breath reeked of stale blood.

"He can't save you," Judd said from behind the light. Headlights. My mom's van, idling. Judd stepped out in front of the light and one of the others, maybe Devon, dragged Danny close and dropped him at my feet. His hands were bound as well. His head lolled to the side and faced me, his eyes closed and mouth agape. I started shouting, tugging and straining against the rope. I screamed for Danny to wake up, to talk to me. I heard my voice echo out. I squinted and made out the shadow of tree branches and saw the moon reflected on rippling water. Back at the goddamned boat ramp.

"End of the line, freak," Judd said, smacking the baseball bat against his palm.

"You're so fucking stupid," I said. That earned a thwack across the face with the baseball bat. I wiggled my jaw, making sure it wasn't broken. It hurt like hell, but I tried to hide it. My mouth flooded with new blood as one of my teeth came loose. "You're all going to hang for this."

"I doubt it," Judd said. "I'm just finishing what I started." There were some snickers from his cohorts. "My daddy said you and your butt buddy here have got the devil in you," Judd said, grabbing my hair in his fist and yanking my head around. "And after your little trick with the bees, I guess you could say I'm a believer."

"Is that the same daddy you cry about at night?" I asked, half paying attention to his dastardly villain bit. I struggled to reach my foot out and grab Danny. Any way to bring him closer to me. "How many times did you fuck Danny before you killed him? Was sending him dick pics all part of your crusade tactics?" I finally managed to snag Danny's shirt and tried to yank him closer. I sensed a hesitation from Judd's friends.

"You're pretty mouthy for a dead man," Judd said.

"You'd be surprised how mouthy the dead can be," I said, rolling Danny closer. I finally managed to get his head between my legs.

"What the fuck are you doing?" Judd asked, watching me struggle.

"Another one of my devil tricks," I said with a bloody grin. I brought my head low and leaned down as far as I could. A thick glob of my spit and blood fell out of my mouth and into Danny's. This earned several shocked "what the fuck"'s from the peanut gallery. Danny's eyes shot open and my stomach dropped. Danny Moreland was not there. Someone or something else had taken the reins. I looked at Judd and found Danny leaning up to look at him too. Was I the thing behind Danny's eyes?

"Get back down, faggot," Judd said and planted his foot in Danny's chest. Danny didn't budge. In the briefest flash of a thought, I imagined Judd dying an agonizing death. I was not careful what I wished for.

The ropes around Danny's wrists whined and cracked as he pulled them apart. He slowly stood, his back arched and he held his hands out, fingers splayed like claws. "What are you waiting for?" Judd asked Devon and Liam.

What followed was a fantastic shadow play. Devon stepped into the light, bringing a tire iron down over his head. Danny caught it as it swung down and used his other hand to grab Devon around the throat.

Devon coughed and kicked as Danny raised him into the air. Danny wrenched the tire iron from his hand. Liam went to tackle Danny, but Danny swung the tire iron with a shocking swiftness. There was a thud and a gut-wrenching crunch as the metal bar was buried in Liam's skull. Another thud as Liam hit the dirt. Judd screamed, backing into the hood of the van. Devon struggled until Danny's grip grew so tight his neck snapped. Danny tossed him onto the ground. Judd shouted as he swung the bat against Danny's head. The bat shattered into splinters, cascading out into the night. Danny grabbed Judd and whirled, throwing him down at my feet.

"Danny! No! Please, Humphrey, you gotta stop him," Judd pleaded, arching his head back to look up at me.

"Fuck off," I said and spit a streak of red and pink across his face. Danny approached, his form in silhouette growing larger by the second. Judd tried to scramble back and I found him pushing against my chest, kicking his feet out in panic.

Danny knelt down and drew close. Judd was whimpering, asking for forgiveness. "It was just a joke!"

he tried to say. Danny placed his face against Judd's neck. He looked up at me and I only saw the blazing green light of my miracle liquid in his pupils. His teeth rested against Judd's pulsing neck and he paused, as if waiting for my permission. I nodded. "Please!" Judd shouted. "Please!"

Danny's teeth shredded through Judd's neck. He screamed and spasmed as Danny took big bites of his flesh. Danny's face was painted slick and red. Both of us were splattered by the spray jutting from Judd's jugular. It was warmer than the early summer air. The smell was suffocating, rust and piss mixing as Judd's fear spilled out into the night. Judd's hands had formed fists, balling up my dress pants. His cries turned into soggy gurgles. Eventually, his muscular body went slack. For that's all he was, then. A lifeless body. A pig butchered.

I tried to ask Danny to move Judd off of me, but he snarled. One would do well not to interrupt a tiger's meal, certainly. So we sat that way for a while, Judd's body pressing against me as Danny bit and tore and chewed select body parts. Through it all, the sound seemed to mystify me most. The horror movies had all gotten it wrong. It was wet cloth being torn from top to tip. It was sinew pulled so taut it snapped with a twang. It was delighted grunts muffled by wet muscle. All with an overture of bone on bone as teeth hurried to pulverize anything in their path.

It wasn't comfortable, but I didn't mind all that much. My brain produced the incredibly unhelpful thought that we certainly weren't returning our tux rentals. The red soaked up and through every inch of Danny's suit and shirt as he busily slurped and slopped.

If nothing else, it gave me time to think about what to do with the bodies.

Graduation rolled around faster than we could have anticipated. Time flies when you're covering up a multiple murder. There were rumors, of course. But no one blabbed to anyone that mattered. To no one's surprise, three varsity athletes going missing the night of prom was a big deal. But between our cunning and the police's ineptitude, it seemed we had pulled it off. I had let Danny get his fill, and then we staged the bodies in Judd's muscle car and sent it flying off a cliff down into the lake. No one was wearing seatbelts, of course. The windows were open. There were beer cans and plastic vodka bottles. Water does awful things to bodies. Catfish, gar, and snapping turtles are known to eat just about anything that will fit in their mouths. The authorities surely found human teeth marks on some of their bones, but if they had, we never heard about it.

The last day of our school year was set aside for grieving. I wore a white shirt and black tie to school. Danny was furious. He hated me in general those days. When he came to, caked in viscera and dirt, he wanted to do the right thing, call the police, an ambulance. Maybe one of them could make it out alive. But cooler heads, namely mine, prevailed. He sobbed and wretched as we did our dirty work. I didn't want to tell him, but in the moonlight, his stomach full, he was practically radiant. The healthiest I had seen him look in ages.

I still think of that night sometimes. Not really the blood and guts. The aftermath. Maybe the closest we had ever been or ever would be. The closest I'd be to another human for the rest of my life. Maybe being accomplices is more intimate than being in a relationship. I really wouldn't know.

Once we had done the deed, we stripped out of our suits and stuffed them into bags that had amassed in my mom's floorboards. By this point, he was well and truly checked out. That was fine. He had done all the hard work, so now it was time for me to pull my weight too. I would be alert and think of all the stupid little things murderers often forget.

I put a towel down across the backseat for Danny to lay on. I drove us back to my house. We rode with the windows down, the cool air washing over our naked bodies. I reached back and Danny took hold of my hand. The blood was cold and sticky now, sealing our fingers together. I reassured him that everything was going to be okay.

When we got to my house, I drove the van past the end of the driveway, out to the treeline. We made a fire and burned all of our clothes. I watched him watching the fire, the flames dancing in his eyes. Among the trees, fireflies glowed green in the darkness. Or maybe it was my bee friends.

I laid my head on his shoulder and he rested his on mine. We both took big breaths. There was still so much to do.

After everything had burned, we walked back to the house. We stepped into the shower and washed away the smoke and the blood. He seemed to melt in the hot water. I scrubbed Danny's hands and arms until they were pink. He looked into my eyes as I cleaned his face, humming a little tune as I worked. Danny's breath hitched in his throat and he began to cry. "It's alright," I said, drawing his head down onto my chest. "You're alright." He gripped my back so hard it bruised, but I held him close until long after the water went cold.

Everyone cried during the assembly. Judd's dad came and talked about how Judd would want anyone not saved by Jesus to pray with him right then and there and give themselves over to the Lord. I couldn't help but grin. His shitstain of a son died because he killed my best friend, then tried to kill us both. To say I lacked remorse was…an understatement.

Summer came on quick. We walked the line. My mom wondered why Danny and I weren't celebrating our graduation together. I said he was nervous about college. We had both been accepted to Miskatonic after all. My scores weren't spectacular, but I felt I could improve and eventually earn an MD. I had had so much experience with biological processes over that year, it seemed I had a knack for it.

As I've mentioned, Danny and I were no strangers to fights from time to time. But we always calmed down and made amends. This particular gap between fighting and friendship was getting a little long. I was mostly worried that he wasn't getting any sustenance. I tried to bring him some, but he wouldn't come to the door.

One day, he came over unannounced. We went to the cellar for what would be our final chat. "I'm not going to MU," Danny said. The prom night feast seemed to still be doing him some good. He didn't look pale or malnourished.

"I wish you would have told me that," I said, exasperated. "I didn't get accepted anywhere else. Where are you going?"

"Nowhere," Danny said. There were tears in his eyes. "I can't go out into the world like this. Just to hurt or kill more people."

"Hey," I said, coming close to hug him, "we'll figure something out." Danny recoiled a few steps. "Are you still feeling guilty over Judd?" I asked and I couldn't hide my exasperation. He flinched at the name and looked up the stairs to make sure no one was listening.

"There's nothing to feel bad about," I said, lowering my voice. "It was kill or be killed. You did the right thing."

"I mean, yeah, maybe," he said, agonizing. "But killing and…and," he looked at me with disdain, "eating someone are two different things."

"You have to crack a few eggs to make an omelet," I said with a shrug. This was not the right thing to say. Not in the slightest.

"How did I never see it before?" he asked. I asked him what he meant. "You're fucking evil." He scoffed in disbelief. I hardly thought that was fair.

"I think that's subjective-" I began.

"You don't have a soul," he said, getting close. "You're a hateful little prick who wants to play God."

"I would argue no one has a soul," I said. "We're just meat machines that work until we don't." He looked at me bewildered. "Regardless, are you going to turn yourself in?" I asked, crossing my arms. "Is that it? Let's go, I'll take the van. We'll add it to my list of charges." Danny started to cry and pull at the sides of his hair. "If I could have done it, I would have. But your closetcase boyfriend had me tied up pretty good. With the intent to murder me, might I add."

"Is that what it's about?" Danny asked. "Are you jealous?"

"Of that waste of breath? Hardly," I said, rolling my eyes. I squinted at him. "Do you miss him?" I asked mockingly, meaning it as a joke. I smiled, but he didn't.

"What is your fucking problem?" he asked. This struck a nerve. All I could think was that it was over. We had made it out. After four years of torture, we won. It was like all of our, my, hard work had been for nothing.

"Danny, let's not kid ourselves," I said. "If the roles were reversed, you wouldn't have done any of this for me. I'd be yet another dead queer swept under the rug. I didn't want that for you."

"Come off it," he said. "You didn't even give me a choice. That night, with Judd and the others...I tasted you. I could only hear your voice in my head. I didn't hear them scream or hear their bones break. I only heard you, telling me - forcing me to do it!"

"You may not remember it," I said levelly, "but after you stopped them, what you did to them after that, that wasn't me. No matter how you feel, it doesn't change the fact of the matter. You wanted to eat them."

"I'm not a monster!" he screamed. "I'm not a statement piece. I...I don't know what I am anymore. But I'm not your puppet to get revenge on people who bully you."

"Bullied. Past tense," I said resolutely. "And I never said you were any of those things," I tried to reason with him. I'd gone too far, but I could salvage it. Best friends don't stay mad forever. "If you don't want to go to school, fine. I won't either." I gave him a smile, but it didn't seem to work. "Here, I bet you're hungry," I said, moving to the fridge. I had amassed a little stockpile. He looked at the vial in my hand and then back at me.

"Humphrey," Danny said, a tear dropping from his eye. "Please never speak to me again." He turned and climbed the stairs. I chased him, the blood still in my hand.

"Wait!" I said, following him out onto the gravel driveway. I had to sprint, damn my short legs, but I caught up to him right before he stepped out onto the road. I grabbed his shoulder and he wheeled around. He shoved me back so hard it knocked the wind out of me. I fell back into the gravel and groaned. My hands were scraped, and the vial was scratched, but it didn't shatter. I twisted off the top and held it up to him. "Please," I said. "I'm sorry. I'm sorry about all of it. Let me take care of you." A sob racked his body and he covered his face.

"I'm serious," he said, turning away. "Don't come near me. Leave me alone."

"I promise," I said. "I'll burn all my research. I'll never tell you what to do again!" I cried, watching him walk away. I didn't budge from that spot for a few minutes. I called after him, but he disappeared into his house with a slam of his front door.

And that was the last I saw of Danny Moreland.

I stayed my course to university and did achieve my MD. There was always a part of me that hoped he would come around. He knew where I'd be, whenever he was ready. However, he never felt inclined to do so.

I did try to burn mine and H.W.'s notes as I had promised. But in the moment, I felt compelled to save them. I used my own hand to fish the book out of the fire and put out the flames. Still have a patch of rippled, scarred flesh to prove it. Whatever ideals I had over who owned what, that journal held, still holds, me captive, not the other way around. I placed it in the box I had mentioned earlier, but it whispers to me sometimes. A high, reedy voice that reminds me that there are still pages to be filled. Tells me to carry on with the research I had started. During my undergrad, I saw plenty of people who would have benefitted from my creation. But I resisted the temptation. Whatever came back to life would be my responsibility, and I had failed enough for one lifetime.

From the beginning, I told you Danny was never far from my thoughts. I wonder about him constantly. Now that some time has passed, I wonder if he's aged at all. I wonder if he found flesh and blood to consume. If he had stuck with me I could have gotten him cadaver flesh at the very least. We carved up so many bodies over the years that just went to waste.

I can say, there are times he's so pervasive in my thoughts that I think I see him. It's always in the dark, of course, where identities are easy to mistake. But every so often, even more-so since I began writing this down and dredging up old memories, I look over my shoulder to find him crossing the street or turning to go into a shop. Recently, the mistaken individual or spectral figure, whichever it may be, has gotten closer and closer. Wishful thinking, perhaps. What would I do if it were him? Wrap him up in a hug? Would we pretend none of it had ever happened? Just two old high school buddies, picking up where they left off.

I saw "him" just tonight on my way home, as a matter of fact. Tall, pale, with dazzling eyes and blood red lips. All this ancient history seems to be haunting me. I've got myself riled up again. Even now, I can look out my window and see him standing in my yard. He's looking up at my window. Hungry and tired out there in the snow. I had better go let him in

You & Me & The Devil Makes Three

George had been living under the sink for some time. Or so Alan Jr. believed. His mom, Rosemary, sloshed the water around as she stood washing dishes. As had been their custom for weeks, maybe even a few months Alan estimated, she was muttering and he was whispering back. "The nerve of that man!" Rosemary said, carelessly tossing silverware over onto the rack with a clang. "I say we do it tonight. Are you strong enough, you think?"

Alan Jr. did his best to sneak up to the kitchen to eavesdrop. He watched his mom's back, her ladybug patterned housedress protected by an apron. None of the lights were on and the blinds were closed tight. He kept catching his mama talking in the kitchen, which she kept as dark as possible. Alan Jr. couldn't be positive how long it had been going on, since he had been in school, but now that it was summer, he was at home to hear it happen.

At first he had assumed she was just talking or singing songs to herself. But it had become clear that wasn't the case. There was an intended audience: George. "Oh, George. Don't tell me you're on his side all of a sudden," Rosemary said when "George" (whoever he was) did not offer his opinion.

Alan Jr. thought back to his imaginary friend Neil. It didn't seem right, but maybe adults had invisible friends too and they were too embarrassed to talk about it. He knew his mama in particular didn't have many friends, no book clubs or bridge games like his friends' moms. She got invited, but would say Alan Senior wouldn't like it. Alan Jr. knew that wasn't just an excuse.

Alan Jr. held his breath and leaned in closely, straining to hear. The floor had given him away several times before. His mom seemed to be in the kitchen more often than not. Had she always spent this much time there without him realizing? The last time she kept watch over a closet or cupboard this closely, it was where she had hidden his Christmas presents.

Alan Jr. got the distinct impression this was not a pleasant surprise she was guarding.

Loud scrapes of fork against plate rang out as Rosemary raked some toast and eggs, a cigarette butt sticking out of the mound, down below the sink. Alan Jr. took the opportunity to deftly step closer, inching his face past the door frame.

A low rumble creeped out from the cabinet, one of its doors still ajar. "Don't be stupid," Rosemary said, wiping at her forehead with her arm. "That boy will sleep until noon if I let him. A drop of sweat from him would cure cancer," she said. "He gets that from his daddy," she added with disdain. The rumble came again, causing sudsy cups and saucers to clink together. Rosemary turned her head to see Alan Jr., who wasn't quick enough. The way she looked at him, exhaustion carved into her face, her eyes flat and unfocused, she didn't look like his mama at all. This only lasted a split second before her mouth turned up into a smile, like the strings on a puppet were pulled taut. "Good morning, sweetie!" Rosemary said, her voice jumping up from its comfortable murmur.

"Who were you talking to?" Alan Jr. asked, hazarding a step into the kitchen. Maybe it was best to try a direct approach.

"Just myself," Rosemary said, shrugging. "You know your silly old mama."

Alan Jr. moved towards the sink. He hunkered down, trying to peer into the darkness. Something shiny caught what little light came into the room. Whatever it was moved and the cabinet door slammed shut, causing Alan Jr. and Rosemary to jump. "You have to stay out of there!" Rosemary shouted. She held a knife in her rubber gloved fist, soap sliding down its edge and dripping onto the floor. "There's all kinds of chemicals and bleach I use for cleaning. You have to be careful, that's all," Rosemary said with an unconvincing smile. She tossed the knife into the water and peeled the gloves off with a snap.

They stood in silence for a moment, Alan Jr. trying to find something else to say. "Why don't I make you some breakfast and then you can go see what your friends are up to." She kissed him on the top of his head and busied herself cracking and scrambling eggs. "Go to sleep, you little baby," she sang over the sizzle of the skillet. There was a time she would sing the tune to him while he drifted into sleep. Alan Senior had put an end to it, saying she was coddling him. Making him soft. Alan Jr. missed it terribly. "Don't need nobody but the baby," Rosemary half sang, half hummed.

While his mind had strayed slightly, Alan refused to look away from the cabinet. After a minute or two, Rosemary stepped between him and the cabinet, setting the plate down in front of him. He had an idea. "Mama," he said, poking at the eggs. Rosemary grew rigid, clenching her fists, waiting for him to continue. "Can you call Mrs. Carpenter and see if I can spend the night with Joey?"

"That's an excellent idea!" Rosemary said, seemingly happy at the prospect of having him out of the house. The heels of her shoes clicked across the floor as she went to the living room to use the phone. Alan Jr. carefully laid his fork down and as quietly as he could, pushed himself away from the table. "Yes, operator?" his mom asked into the phone. When it was clear she had gotten through to Mrs. Carpenter, Alan Jr. bolted for the cabinet below the sink. He pulled one door open, praying the hinges wouldn't cry out.

Beyond the jumble of brightly colored bottles and cans of cleaning solutions, the tiny space was nothing but shadow. He reached out a hand, swallowing hard to get his heart back down into his chest. Screwing his eyes closed, he delved deeper and deeper. His breath hitched as his fingers touched something. Alan Jr. fidgeted his fingers, fumbling about, and found nothing but the back wall. He felt foolish. What could possibly have been under there? He softly closed the cabinet door again, wrestling with what this meant. Maybe his mama just had a quirk. Lots of people did, he was finding out as he got older. He wondered if the doctor had given her any more of the rusty red pills and if she had been taking them.

There was click-clacking against the floor again, so Alan Jr. jumped up and reached for his plate, meaning to justify how close he was to the sink. A shockwave of goosebumps rippled down his arms and legs as something slithered out of sight beneath the kitchen table. He stepped back, bumping against the counter. This jolted him, making him drop the plate. It fell to the floor and shattered in a gunshot crack. Alan shook his head, trying to make sense of what he saw. He'd have to tell his mom to get some rat traps. But he couldn't shake the sensation, the knowledge. Rats didn't have dozens of spindly legs, unlike whatever had just skittered away.

"Alan Michael!" his mom called from the living room. But she wasn't scolding him for the broken plate. There was fear in her voice. He looked to her as the cabinet beside his leg creaked open a little wider. He closed his eyes, forcing himself not to look down. He made to move away. There was a commotion as the bottles beneath the sink flew out into the kitchen and something struck out at him like a snake. Alan screamed as pincers sunk into the flesh of his calf, yanking his leg and causing him to hit the ground. Rosemary ran to his side.

"Mom? Mom!" Alan yelled, clawing at her apron. She grabbed hold of his arms and leaned back, trying to tug him free. This only dug the pincers deeper, blood running down in rivulets, flowing out into the grout grooves between the tiles.

"George, stop it!" Rosemary yelled at the thing from beneath the sink. George's many clustered, burnt lightbulb eyes danced with glee. The segments of its body shone black like new shoes, inlaid with swooping ridges that looked sharp to the touch. From between the pincers that held Alan Jr. tightly, George's mouth unfolded. Two fangs drew up, ready to sink into the boy's skin. George's antennae roved along his shin, looking for the best place to bite, yanking out hairs as they waved about. Rosemary screamed as the serrated, obsidian sickle fangs punctured Alan's leg. Alan cried out, reaching up and grabbing hold of one of George's antennae, meaning to yank it out. However, his hands went lax and he fell back with a thud.

"I-I can't feel it, mama. Why can't I feel it?" Alan Jr. sputtered. The mixture of adrenaline and neurotoxin stunned him and slurred his speech. His heart slammed against his ribs. Rosemary screamed at George to stop.

"Don't you wish to be free?" George asked in a whisper. "This is why you kept me. Fed me fat meats. Told me their sins."

"Not him," Rosemary said frantically. "We had a deal!" Alan Jr.'s vision began to blur and he felt his chest growing tight. The numb pressure against his leg loosened and he felt little pinpricks traveling up his thighs, as if his legs were asleep. He strained to look down at his belly. George skittered up Alan Jr.'s abdomen, its sewing needle legs gripping the fabric of his shirt, tearing tiny holes as it stepped. George grew closer, bringing its face close to his. In its glistening cake bell eyes, Alan Jr. was multiplied, dozens of boys laid flat and bleeding, gasping at the ceiling.

Rosemary slipped a hand between them and ushered George back, like you might a dog being overly curious. She held George's grotesque head in her hands much the same. "I'll keep my promise," Rosemary said, "I swear it." She leaned forward and kissed its face, a smudge of red lipstick left behind on its black shell. Alan Jr. struggled to breathe as his sight began to narrow to a pinpoint. Down to a single red and black bug on his mama's apron.

Alan Jr. couldn't be sure how long he was out. His mind clawed back out of the loamy earth of dreams to see his dad kneeling over him. "Good lord, woman," he said to Rosemary, who stood by the sink. Alan Jr. could smell booze on his father's breath and wrinkled his nose at it. "Where the hell's the doctor? Tell me you're not so stupid you forgot to call the doctor." Alan Jr. tried to speak, tried to lift his arm to point at the cabinet that his mama stooped to open fully. "Hush, son," his father said. "Save your-"

A stroke of dark lightning streaked across the room. George was on Alan Senior. Alan Jr. began to drift away again as George wound itself tightly around Alan Sr., covering his mouth with its hideous bulk. His father's face grew red, his eyes wide and bulging. Rosemary came to sit between Alan Jr. and the tangled mass that was George subduing its prey.

Alan Sr.'s hand shot out and grabbed hold of Rosemary's forearm, finding a familiar patch of skin where the same hand had gripped so many times before. Rosemary brushed it away and smiled. Her whole body seemed to relax, as if she were made of clockwork springs so tightly wound, finally able to come undone. She looked to Alan Jr. and saw his eyes brimming over with tears. "Look away, sweetheart," Rosemary said, gently nudging his face so he looked at the far wall. He could still see the shadows of what was happening. The single silhouette split as George reared up, stretching and spilling up onto the ceiling. In an instant he plunged back down again. Flecks of something warm splashed onto Alan Jr.'s neck.

Crunches and wet squelches filled the kitchen. There was the sound of polished shoes scraping across the floor, attached to flailing legs. After what felt like forever, the legs finally stopped. The kitchen became quiet, aside from the soft sound of meat being minced. Finally, Rosemary let out a contented sigh.

"You sure are a messy eater," Rosemary said and giggled. Alan Jr. didn't know she was capable of giggling. The astringent smell of bleach washed over Alan Jr. and his eyes flickered. Rosemary grunted as she pushed Alan Jr. towards the wall, away from the "mess". She ran her fingers through his hair and hummed for a moment. "Come lay your bones on the alabaster stones," Rosemary sang out loud as she receded back to her task, "and be my ever-lovin' baby."

Alan Jr. woke up after a little slice of eternity. Every beat of his heart pounded in his head. He heard his mama muttering. A low, grinding voice answered in a whisper. Alan Jr. groaned in fear and Rosemary was at his side instantly. "Oh, thank God," she said, brushing his hair away from his forehead.

"You had a nasty bite, son," an old man in a white coat said. More of the room seemed to pour in from the darkness and Alan Jr. realized he was in the hospital. "I'd say a brown recluse, but I'm no expert."

"I'll let you two talk," a policeman said from the foot of his bed. "We'll let you know if we have any more questions about Alan Senior-" he said, then halted. "Best for you to be the one," he said to Rosemary and tipped his hat. He and the doctor left, shutting the door behind them. Alan Jr. looked to his mama and she smiled. Perhaps the most genuine smile he had ever seen on her. It was easy and weightless.

"I'm so happy you're okay," she said. She gripped his hand in hers and squeezed it tightly. "I have some bad news," Rosemary said, and it was clear to Alan Jr. she was acting. Like a movie star at the drive-in, she looked away and put on a brave face. "Your father is missing. They're doing everything they can to find him." She heaved a big breath that hitched in her throat as a single tear raced down her cheek. "All we can do is pray," she said towards the door where shadows still lingered just outside.

Alan Jr. gripped the sheets of the bed, his mouth still unable to cooperate. He desperately wanted to scream. To alert someone, anyone, to what was happening. Rosemary's concerned face began to change. Her eyes went beetle-shell black. The skin of her forehead split open to reveal more and more eyes, bundled together. From inside her mouth, two slender pincers came, dripping with drool.

"I know it will take some getting used to," Rosemary's gentle voice mixed with George's whisper. They were joined together now, married in flesh. "But it will just be the three of us from now on."

THE WANTING

Walter's Wanting came fairly late in life. As far as Wanting's go, it was quiet and unobtrusive, much like him. He woke, his head full of dreams. Skin and mouths.

Slipping out of the bed he slept in alone, he shuffled into the kitchen to get a glass of water. He looked up from filling his cup to see his Wanting. A faint red light spilled out of the barely open barn door. Moths fluttered past the light, uninterested in its glow. No, he thought, it was just meant for him. His cup was now running over, spilling water down his hand.

He came out from under the spell of the light and turned off the tap. Walter took big gulps of the water, hoping to quench the sick feeling that now gripped him. This couldn't be right. He was still half-awake, his mind playing tricks.

Walter returned to bed and shut the door firmly. Laying there, he could still see the light. It crawled under the door. It reached up at his bedskirt, unable to quite climb higher. Walter shut his eyes tightly and rolled away.

The morning came and the light was gone, as far as he could tell. He was being foolish, he thought to himself. No grown man gets his Wanting. That was kid stuff. Maybe if he was some young pup, but even back then he knew how to control himself.

His parents had been so proud he had made it through high school without a Wanting. That was extremely rare for boys. At least that's what "they" said. His parents had a habit of only listening to "them" when it suited their needs. But in this case, he had seen it. Walter had hung around the outside of locker room chats where boys compared their Wantingmarks, bragged about how they got 'em. Most of his graduating class had the telltale bone-deep blemish somewhere on their person. No matter the color of their skin, their Wantings marked them with the same crimson color,

burning bright and angry red. Walter had always
wondered if it hurt, but couldn't bring himself to ask
even those closest to him. His best friend Jimmy. The
neighbor boy, Michael McGinnis.

While his coffee brewed he thought back to that
night. The night Michael McGinnis gave in to his
Wanting. The McGinnises had lived just down the road
a ways. Walter was going to bed late. He had just
finished watching some show about aliens taking over
the world. So he didn't think twice when he saw the red
light in the night, way off at the McGinnises. Just
another strange thing to have seen. But as the gray blue
tint of the T.V. wore away from his mind, he realized
what was happening. He stood at his window, the same
room he slept in now, staring out at the light. Walter had
brought his hand up to the window and touched it,
expecting to feel something...maybe heat from the light.
But it was only as warm as the air outside. He thought
of Michael McGinnis. A nice guy. Maybe a little wilder
than Walter. Jumped off tall rocks down into the creek.
Climbed any tree, you didn't even have to dare him.
Things like that.

A shadow moved in front of the light and

stopped. It was impossible to know, but he felt whoever or whatever it was was staring back at him. Smiling.

Walter dropped to the floor, clamping his eyes shut and his hand over his mouth to keep from screaming out loud. He spent the rest of the night with his head hidden beneath the covers, despite the summer heat.

The next day and for a couple days after that, the police came to ask them questions. Had any of them been acting suspiciously? Did Michael mention or say anything out of the ordinary? Walter had told them everything he could think of. He asked the policeman when he could see Michael. Walter remembered the weight of his dad's hand on his shoulder, how it patted him piteously. He didn't truly know nothing about Wantings then.

But once he was old enough to understand his momma told him what had happened. It made him feel sick. Michael couldn't have done something like that. On her prescription, he had sat down to talk with Pastor Alan about it. Walter could still hear the disgust in the old preacher's voice. "If you ever get to feeling that way," he said, "you tell somebody. And you pray to God to take it away from you." Pastor Alan always wore white felt gloves and all these years later, Walter had an inkling why. He never saw his parents' or his teachers' Wantingmarks, but thought that was likely for the best. Walter's mind wandered away like smoke from a house fire.

That's when the phone calls started. Walter jumped out of his trip down memory lane as the receiver hopped around, the little bell inside the phone crying out with all its might. "Ward residence," Walter said brusquely. There was silence on the line. No, not silence. Whoever it was wasn't speaking, but Walter knew they were there. "Hello?" he asked. Whoever was on the other end took a deep breath. It seemed to go on for an hour. "Well say something," Walter almost yelled. A long breath out. A moan. Walter slammed the phone down back onto its hooks. The rotary dial looked up at him with its 10 little eyes. Walter stood by the phone for another minute, but it didn't ring again.

He got his coffee and stepped out onto the front porch in his boxers. Nobody lived around here anymore. Walter could walk around naked as a jaybird if he really wanted to. He sipped his coffee that was still a little too hot, still mad over the prank caller. Sicko. Pervert.

Walter looked to where the McGinnis house had been. The yard had grown up and before long, the white boards couldn't be seen for the creeping vines. No one in their right mind would live where such a thing had happened. Walter scanned the rolling hills, dotted with cows that drifted by as lazily as the clouds. He found himself staring over at the barn. The door was still ajar, but only by a hair. He must have left it unlocked. Better go make sure nothing got stole, he thought to himself. He went back in, put down his coffee, put on his boots and traipsed out over the gravel.

The phone began to ring again.

Walter turned, half expecting the phone to be outside with him, it sounded so loud. He watched the kitchen window for a minute, but decided to let it ring. Didn't do any good to answer those prank callers, to give 'em what they wanted. Just some stupid kids, he bet. Walter stepped close to the barn and froze.

The door was now shut and locked. He tugged at the padlock, but found it firmly clasped. Hands on his hips, he tried to figure how this could've happened.

The ringing of the telephone kept him from thinking clearly. He stomped back into the house and yanked the handle up to his ear. "Now you better have something to say," Walter said, doing his best John Wayne hardass growl.

"Well, Walt," he heard Jimmy say from the other end. "I didn't think you'd still be asleep at this hour." Walter let out a sigh. All this thinking about Wantings had him remembering how Jimmy had given in to his as well. He thought of Jimmy's legs and how they had turned the color of cardinal wings. Walter's mind filled with an image he tried to shake free. How far up did the red stain go, he wondered.

Though he had not had his Wanting, he was no stranger to its many, many children. Yearning, pining, wishful thinking. They had all gnawed on him with coyote teeth for some time now. Chewed on his gristle and licked out his marrow.

"Sorry, Jimmy," Walter said, short of breath. "I've had some prank callers this morning."

"Don't be too harsh. We were known to

117

ding-dong ditch in our day," James said, chuckling.
Walter squeezed his eyes shut and pinched the bridge of
his nose. "I was wondering if today would be alright to
come 'round and look at that tractor," Jimmy.said.
Walter opened his eyes, still seeing swirls and bursts of
color.

"Sure thing," Walter said, distracted. He slowly
dropped the phone from his ear as he looked out the
window. The barn door was open again. Even in the
morning sun, he could see the red light coming from
the shadows. Jimmy's voice drifted from the dangling
phone, asking if Walter was still there.

Cows now crowded near the fence, standing in
silence, watching him closely. Walter's footsteps
crunched over the gravel as he crossed to the barn door.
The lock lay on the ground, yanked clean from its loop.
Walter reached a hand out and felt a gust of wind race
up along the ground and up his legs. It urged him
forward. The red light fell across his eye as he peered
inside. His pulse thumped against his throat.

A pile of hay in the corner was littered with
arms and legs. The Wanting's crimson turned the flesh
pink and coral. Walter felt something grip his stomach

and weigh heavy in his groin. His mouth parched, he stumbled forward through the open door.

A copy of Walter laid stark naked in the hay, wet and smiling. The hair all along his body was slicked down to the skin and stray bits of hay stuck to whatever coated him.

"Hey, Walter," the hay him said from the ground with a grin. Walter began to harden, pushing against the fly of his boxers. He tried to cover himself with his hands.

"You can't be in here!" Walter shouted.

"Too late," the other replied, and Walter could swear it was Jimmy's voice. He stretched contentedly, like a cat in the sun.

"What are you?" Walter asked breathlessly. He knelt down in the dirt. The other him opened his legs wide, not an ounce of shame anywhere.

"Whatever you want," the other Walter said. "Yours for the taking." In the red light, it was as if his gums were bleeding down onto the teeth Walter saw every morning in the mirror. Walter hazarded a touch along the other Walter's leg. He was warm and let out a laugh.

"I shouldn't-" Walter said, but his hand continued to travel upward. A shuddering wave passed over him and he gripped the other Walter's thigh, trying to prove that he didn't exist. But to his dread delight, he found it was all too real.

"Come here," the other Walter said, leaning up and pulling Walter down on top of him. Walter desperately drug his lips across the other's. Their tongues met and Walter did his best to ignore his need for breath. The other him tasted like cut grass and honeysuckle, with a slight tang of busted lip. Trying hard not to break the embrace, Walter tugged at his boxers, pulling them down past his knees. Both of them gasped sharply.

Walter didn't hear Jimmy's truck come up the drive, or the door that creaked and slammed shut. Walter was too busy looking into his own eyes, dazzling darkly in the Wanting's light, slightly obscured by a smile.

"Walt?" Jimmy asked as he stepped inside the barn. Walt spun around. Jimmy was silhouetted against the sun, making Walt hold up a hand.

The red light was gone and so was his other self.

Walt sat back into the hay. Jimmy watched him closely, checking over his shoulders suspiciously. Walt made no move to pull his boxers back up. Jimmy stammered, his cheeks burning. "I should come back later," he said, but didn't move. "Y-You alright?"

Walter extended a hand, its palm a solid shade of bloody red. This same color was brushed along his chest and belly where they had pressed against the other Walter. He glistened in the sliver of light from the open door. "Never better," Walt said. "Do you want to join me?"

SNAKEDOCTORS

It was one of the endless days of summer. The humid air and the cicadas' song made me feel like I was drowning while the earth was bone dry. I had been outlawed from my momma's kitchen. She said I was buggin' her, always underfoot. I needed to get out and enjoy the sunshine while I could. The summer never lasts as long as you think, she said.

Roy was similarly sent out into the wilderness and told to come home at dark. So naturally, he wound up at my house. Roy had hit his growth spurt already and had eyes real close like a possum. He had sprouted a few chin hairs and thought that made him my boss. His bike was his bigger (but shorter) brother's hand me down, so his knees nearly came up to his chest as he pedaled up the dusty drive.

"Let's go swim," he said. The sun had brought his freckles to the surface of his cheeks and along his nose.

"I don't know, Roy," I said. "Memaw told me not to go to the crick. It's probably all dried up anyway." I was rereading one of my comic books for the hundredth time, clean-cut GI types exploring distant planets where they didn't belong. Swimming sounded like way more fun, but I took my memaw's words as gospel. The trees talked to her when she sat real still. She always had a plant to pick when you were feeling any kind of way you didn't want to. And she saw spooks that told her things in her dreams while she dozed off in the sunshine. They had told her of the widow Emily Jones and how she lingered at the old bridge where she died, and she may never find rest.

Between the heat and Roy calling me names, I finally gave in. Momma made us some sandwiches and told us to be careful. If we saw a dragonfly, their snake patients were no doubt somewhere nearby. I knew that already, but I told her yes ma'am.

The breeze from riding as fast as we could gave

some relief, but just enough to cool the sweat we were working up to pedal up the hills before coasting down the other side. We took a fork at the new bridge to get to the old one. Wood and mostly upright out of sheer luck, the old bridge had seen much better days. But that was the easiest place to get in and out. We let our bikes fall to the ground and looked down at the crick.

Somehow, despite the lack of rain, it still seemed full, gurgling as it drifted past the stone supports of the bridge. Roy tugged his shirt over his head, revealing his pale white belly and the hard line border of where his sleeves normally covered, his arms and hands like someone else's stuck on. I saw he had what could be classified as chest hairs, and waited for him to gloat. He yanked off his shoes and pulled his socks down, revealing more ghost pale skin.

"Wonder if we'll see her," Roy said as he pulled his shorts off too. I followed suit, knowing a comment about my baby fat would be along shortly.

"Don't say her name," I said, holding up a finger in warning. I spit on the ground as an extra ward against the bad luck he was bringing. Roy stepped out into clear water and let out a big sigh of relief. I followed after him and even though the cool water was a shock, it was exactly what I needed. I dunked my head below the water and looked about at the alien world beneath the surface. I turned about in a circle and realized I didn't see any of the usual frogs or little fish. When I came up for air to tell him, Roy pushed me back down. This happened a few more times, him yanking me up and pushing me back under. Eventually I wiggled my way free and shoved him away. "That ain't funny," I said, but he was obviously tickled. I was so sore I forgot all about the fish.

"Did you think Emily Jones had got you?" he asked, wiggling his fingers.

"You shouldn't...speak ill...of the...dead like that," I said, taking big gulps of air.

"Like what? She killed her babies then herself. Surely there ain't any good way of talking about her. Besides, she's been dead for at least a year," Roy replied, laying on his back and floating a little ways down towards the bridge. "Mikey come here one night and saw her. Said she was cryin'. Serves her right, I reckon." I had heard his brother's story from Roy's mouth no telling how many times.

"That's enough of that," I said and he lifted his head up to look at me so I could see him roll his eyes.

I brought my eyes down level with the water and could see the shadows beneath the bridge were black like a moonless night. And Roy was headed right for them. I brought my head up and swam after Roy. He was grinning up at the sun, his eyes shut like he was sleeping. His face went into the darkness as my hand went out and grabbed his ankle. He jerked upright, but I could barely see him in the dark. I heard the unmistakable sound of a lady crying. We weren't catholic, but I made the sign of the cross like I'd seen some of the kids do.

"What in the hell?" he muttered, his voice carrying up the stones and echoing off the wood. "You gotta-" he was saying before he screamed. He thrashed out towards me and I could see a cloud of red blossoming out under the water. Roy held his hand to his shoulder as he stood and I could see the blood running out from under his fingertips. "Get out of the water!" he yelled at me as he stumbled up the muddy shore. There was a loud splash from under the bridge and I didn't need to be told twice.

Something slick and black green slid upstream towards us. My first reaction was to shout and trip my way up the bank to our bikes. Roy had got to his and was yelling for me to hurry up. His arm hung limply at his waist, a waterfall of red rushing down to where his tan began. Whatever it was broke the surface and two enormous yellow eyes locked onto us. I picked up my bike and held it between me and the thing. It scurried up the bank with no problem, on scrawny legs that lifted up its long body. It was easily as big as a dog. Hell, probably bigger.

I hesitated, thinking we should get our clothes. In that split second, I saw its pinchers spread wide. "Jesus Christ!" I screamed and tried to run for the road. Suddenly, its mouth was moving closer to me. Stretched out on something like a long arm, it grabbed my bike up in its teeth. It yanked my bike free from my hands and I fell on my ass. The bike squealed as the monster crushed its frame between its teeth and then tossed it off into the water.

"Come on!" Roy said, tugging at me. The thing got still, taking aim at us. Roy did the only thing he could think of, I guess, and threw his bike at it too. It grabbed hold of it and didn't waste any time trying to eat his.

We were running down the road, our bare feet slapping the dirt. The thing started chasing us, dripping buckets of water off its body. Something like sobbing came out of the creature, as it called out to us. I picked up the pace, but Roy was starting to wobble, getting woozy from losing blood. I stepped in front of him and had him hold around my neck. I pulled him up onto my back and I ran as fast as I could. The blood from his shoulder ran down onto my mine and he started to whimper, asking for his momma.

We came out of the woods, up to the new bridge. The asphalt scalding my feet, I ran out onto the blacktop. A old pick up truck was hiccuping its way down the road straight towards us. The truck started to honk as the monster came up onto the road. I fell back as its mouth shot out again, getting a hold of my stomach. It was like hot fire as them teeth cut in and took a chunk of me.

The thing was too focused on getting us, I reckon. That pick up truck plowed into that thing and sent it flying out onto the bridge. The old man driving the truck climbed out and pulled the shotgun from its rack in the back window. From the weeds in the ditch, I watched as he hobbled up to it. It cried and cried.

I still swear it tried to say something. I'm not sure what, mind you. But that old man didn't give it the chance, and I can't say as I blame him. The gun went off and echoed out through the trees and fields, sending birds flowing up and out into the sky. I heard the shotgun pumped and then another blast rang out.

I did my best to hold my hand against Roy's shoulder and the other against my belly. The bug, or whatever it was, had taken a plug out of us both. I couldn't stop crying. More for Roy than for me. The doctors said I was in shock, which isn't a surprise. I yelled for the old man and he came. He patted me on the shoulder and said it would all be okay. We loaded Roy into the bed of his truck and I rode back there with him.

There was a tiny bit of a scandal when we first showed up to the hospital. Two near-naked boys covered in blood hobbling through the front doors, me yelling about a bug almost as big as me. The police came and I told them what happened. Roy had lost so much blood they weren't sure if he was going to make it. But he did, the lanky possum he was.

By the time police got to the bridge, whatever it was was gone. The only thing left was a pool of red blood going brown. They didn't believe it was an alien or a bug, or the embodiment of Emily Jones and her drowned babies. But they posted signs all the same, warning people not to swim there. Memaw nursed me back to health, and though she would never say "I told you so," I could feel it in the grins she'd give me when I winced at the rubbing alcohol. When school started back, we had the scars to back up our story. Roy and me were a little braver in our version of the tall tale, but we didn't think that would hurt nothing.

From what I can tell, kids still tell the story of Emily Jones and how she became a demon that ate some stupid boys alive one time. I figure it's better for them to be afraid than to find out themselves.

Nephilim.exe

The lobby of Wavecomm didn't feel like the future to Nessie. It distinctly reeked of the past. How many cigarettes had been smoked here to make the walls that teeth stain color? How many hundreds of heavy footsteps had it taken to wear the carpet down to a shiny streak? She saw the souls of countless employees trudge through the interior door where a guard sat doing crosswords.

Nessie unfolded the newspaper job listing she had cut out. Half of a smiling woman's face was accompanied by the words "SEE, SMELL, TASTE, HEAR, FEEL," in a neat column and then finally "THE FUTURE" in larger letters. "Wavecomm, Riding the Wave of the Future." was printed at the bottom along with their logo. Nessie had interviewed for the position of "operator" listed in the ad and now a few weeks after the fateful acceptance phone call, here she was for her first day. She still wasn't sure exactly what she would be doing, but she knew she was getting paid handsomely for it. The surgery seemed like a drastic step. But again, she thought of the zeroes that would be on her bi-weekly paychecks.

Her head itched like she had lice, but she couldn't scratch any of the spots. The surgeon had told her even the slightest nudge could do some serious damage before the ports healed properly.

A woman looking like she had crawled out of a perfume commercial poked her head out from the door by the security guard. He smiled at her. She didn't look at him. "Vanessa?" she asked the room with lips the color of a kitchen knife nick. Her hair was a cloud of hairspray sticky curls.

"Here!" Nessie shouted, standing. "That's me, I mean." She adjusted her skirt and concentrated on not letting her ankles roll in her heels. "Vanessa Miles," she said, attempting to be confident, extending a hand to the woman.

"What are you doing with hair?" the woman asked instead of introducing herself. There was a badge around the woman's neck that labeled her as Tiffany.

"It's just a wig," Nessie said, trying to laugh, touching the ends.

"The doc should've told you not to wear wigs or hats. If one of those wig hairs- you know what, nevermind." Nessie stood, frozen to the spot. "Well take it off," Tiffany said impatiently, her acrylics clicking together. Nessie obliged, exposing her buzzed scalp to the cold air of the office. She could feel the dried blood around the metal rings dotting her head and wanted desperately to scratch it off.

"What should I-" Nessie began, but Tiffany told her to leave it with the security guard. He looked as embarrassed as she felt handing it over to him. Tiffany held the door open for Nessie. She dug a cigarette out of her shiny clutch and cursed, rooting around inside the small space. Nessie opened her bag and produced a lighter.

"Oh thank God," Tiffany said, taking it from her. She lit her cigarette and handed the lighter back to Nessie. "This is technically my break, so I gotta smoke and walk and talk," Tiffany said, clamping the cigarette in the corner of her mouth. Their heels clicked down the hallway out of sync as Nessie struggled to keep up. "You'll be in Switchboard F. Once you've been here a while, you can probably move up to client work."

"Is that what you did?" Nessie asked.

"Hell no," Tiffany said with a smoke-laced grimace. "No way I'd get-" she said, motioning to her head, looking with naked disgust at Nessie. They reached a door with a large red F on it that conjured memories of high school. "Good luck!" Tiffany said with a fake squeal. "I'm legally required to mention the documents that you signed waiving any liability from Wavecomm in the incident of accident or injury." She said this quickly like the announcer at the end of radio ads. Tiffany stared at Nessie expectantly and seethed a cloud of gray chimney smoke.

"I remember-" Nessie said. She did remember the stack of sticky-note riddled paperwork she had spent an hour scribbling on. The HR rep had said the most important was the NDA agreement, so Nessie wasn't sure what she should acknowledge.

"Okay great!" Tiffany said and let the smile fade

from her face. There was a ringing from her purse. She produced what looked like the dial of a rotary phone. The three colored curl of the Wavecomm logo was in its center. Tiffany flicked a switch on the side. "What?" she barked at it. A tiny voice mumbled back at her. "Oh for Christ's sake!" she yelled, then turned on her heel. Her voice echoed around the halls as she disappeared around a corner.

Nessie stood in the corridor, shivering. She wanted to feel the prickly hairs that had already started to grow, thought the sensation might be a comfort. Instead, she pulled on the door marked F and stepped inside.

It was hot, dark, and noisy. There was a persistent clacking that filled the air like the plumes of smoke drifting up from all over the room. Cubicles seemed to stretch to the horizon, each with a ghastly green glow. Nessie felt she should be quiet, and so she tiptoed along the aisles and rows. Peeking into the little coves, she saw people with their eyes closed, cables leading out of their heads. Their hands twitched and jerked along keyboards attached to what looked like televisions.

Nessie crept closer to a man whose jaw hung slack. The TV had words crawling from left to right as he typed. A bit of drool ran down the corner of his mouth. Standing still and trying to hold her breath, she heard voices. She leaned in. She almost had her ear pressed to the man's lips. The sound of his tongue pressing up against his teeth almost drowned out the words he was forming. If she wasn't mistaken, he was saying, "help."

"Hey," someone said behind Nessie which made her jump and the cactus needle hairs on her neck stood up straight. The man in the chair's eyes fluttered and he leaned forward. He fixed an offended gaze on Nessie. "Take a chill pill, Clark" the voice said to the man and a hand touched Nessie lightly on her shoulder, which made her jump again. "Sorry! Here," the voice said and flicked on a lamp in a nearby cubicle. In the yellow lamplight stood a mohawked woman with a knowing grin. She introduced herself as Sandy. A thick black cable trailed from Sandy's head, down her back, and along the ground. It snaked around the corner into another cubicle. Nessie could clearly see where the end of the cable disappeared into Sandy's skull. This made

Nessie's hands clench reflexively as her stomach squeezed itself. "Let me guess, Tiffany did your onboarding?" Sandy asked.

"If that's what you call walking me to the door," Nessie said, holding her arm, trying to chuckle. Sandy said that sounded about right. She told Nessie to take a seat and she did so.

The cubicle had a few photos pinned to the walls. They were department store shots. A mom, a dad, and a daughter all in their department store clothes. The dad wore big glasses with thin frames and had a bristly red mustache. "Are you sure I'm not taking anyone's spot?" Nessie asked. Sandy eyed the pictures and clearly knew at least one of their occupants. She started to say something then shook her head.

"Don't worry about it," Sandy said and fiddled with the TV. "Turnover is really high around here," she said as a kind of explanation that didn't make Nessie feel better. "You ever seen a computer before?" she asked, and Nessie was relieved to find out small talk still existed. Nessie said she hadn't aside from on TV or in magazines, but that she had been to typing school for electric typewriters. "Kinda close," she said. "Arcades?"

Sandy asked. Nessie gave her a noncommittal shake of her hand, thrown off by the question. She had been in arcades, sure. But she wasn't getting high scores or anything. "In any case, you're about to be intimately acquainted," Sandy said, unspooling cables that ended in metallic jacks.

"What is it I'm supposed to do?" Nessie asked.

"Right now, just hold still," Sandy said. Sandy circled to Nessie's back and instructed her to tilt her head down. Sandy trailed a finger up to the port at the top of Nessie's spinal column, sending shivers down Nessie's neck and shoulders.

"Are you sure?" Nessie asked, groping behind her until she felt Sandy's wrist. "I don't think they're healed."

Sandy leaned forward to whisper in Nessie's ear. "Don't be scared. Trust me." Nessie let go and lowered her hand back down to the chair's armrest. "You're going to feel something like hitting your funny bone. But all over your body." There was a sharp click as Sandy slid the jack into Nessie's neck. Her whole body erupted in aching tingles and she had the urge to giggle at the shock of pain.

"Well that was freaky," Nessie said, shaking her arms to try and get the pins and needles out. Each of the ports hummed inside her head, like bells all rung in unison.

"Kinda like spiders all over you, huh?" Sandy asked, grinning. Nessie reluctantly agreed. Sandy went about plugging in the rest of the cables, each with their own strange sensations. Rusty tastes and high pitched ringing. Sandy leaned back against the desk, admiring her handiwork. Or maybe just Nessie in general. The thought caused Nessie's cheeks to flush. "You're all set," Sandy said with a thumbs up and Nessie did her best to return the gesture, but found it hard to make her fingers cooperate. "How are you feeling?"

"Strange," Nessie managed to say, but as she thought of more words to say they unraveled and trailed away. "Is this the future?" Nessie found herself asking.

"It sure is," Sandy said. "One day, one of these set ups will be in every home in America. Maybe the world. For now, we've got Uncle Sam and the CIA to thank for these puppies," she slapped the top of the screen. She explained the buttons on the computer, how to run programs. Her fingers cascaded along the keys until the screen showed Nessie's face, blurred by the scanlines until her features had started to bleed together. She thought of the old tintype photos that came out just a little wrong. The smear of light as a face was turned too quickly. Or was it a ghost?

"That's me," Nessie said quietly, seeing her name and personal information laid out like a sheet in a file folder.

"Looks like they've got you on connection-observation. Basically, you'll be connecting calls and listening in for anything worth noting. Wavecomm defines that as anything even remotely Commie. But in reality, they don't want to burn through all these tapes," here she flipped out a tray with a cassette inside and then clicked it back closed. "So if you hear any of them talking about setting off a bomb, you press this record button. Otherwise, just connect the caller to the right person in the database and that's that." Nessie felt her face express confusion in every way it could, brows pushing together and a sideways frown on her lips.

"Is that legal?" Nessie asked. "I mean listening in other people's conversations?" Sandy studied Nessie's face to see if she was joking.

Sandy laughed anyway. "You're cute," Sandy said with a wink, then turned back to the computer. Sandy pressed a few more keys and the screen flickered between different lists. Along the top it now read "***CONN-OBS***" "When you're ready, hit the enter key. The computer and your brain will take care of the rest."

"I'm not sure-" Nessie said haltingly.

"If you weren't smart you wouldn't have gotten the job," Sandy said and patted Nessie on the shoulder. "Just take it easy, you'll get the hang of it." Sandy slipped a hand into her shirt and produced a flat square of plastic. "And once you do, you can take a crack at this." The word "Nephilim" was scrawled on a label in black marker. Sandy laid it beside the keyboard.

"What's that?" Nessie asked. She tried to sound out the word in her head, having never seen it before.

"The future," Sandy said with a wry smile. "Strictly underground. We're not supposed to have it, so if Tiffany or anyone else from upstairs asks about a 'disk', you don't have a clue." Nessie nodded and said that wouldn't be hard, since she really didn't have a clue.

Sandy turned the lamp off and the cubicle was draped in shadow again, aside from the monitor's glow. Sandy flowed away in the darkness, leaving Nessie alone with the computer, the holes in her head getting hot and uncomfortable.

Nessie leaned forward and pressed the enter key. Her breath caught in her chest as her body fell back against the chair. Her eyes rolled back in her head and her arms fell away on either side of her. Everything went black. Squares of colored light began as pinpricks in the darkness and came together to form lines and shapes. The sound of a ringing phone came from where her right hand should be. Nessie looked down and saw a face with a name and some numbers. The phone continued to ring.

"Pick it up, already!" Clark said beside her. Or she was pretty sure that's who it was. The lines and spots that hung in the void resembled him, anyway. He gestured to the pictures in front of her. Nessie touched the picture on the right and heard the chaos of a busy street.

"Hello? Operator?" the picture said. "I paid too damn much-"

"Yes! How…can I help you?" Nessie asked.

"Connect me to AL-VA-REZ, JOR-DAN," the picture yelled, trying to be distinct. "ID, oh shit, um." the crinkling of paper came across. "ID 4320, Extension 23. Got that?" they asked.

"Yes? Uh, one moment please," Nessie said, trying to adopt the voice she had used at the perfume counter in what felt like an entirely different life. Near her left hand another picture appeared, the name "Alvarez, Jordan" beneath it, along with the numbers the caller had provided. She touched that picture and the line rang again. A green line like a neon sign appeared between the two pictures as the ringing stopped.

"Yeah?" the picture on her left asked.

"Jordan? It's Petey-" the voice on her right said. Nessie sat quietly and listened. While it didn't feel right, it did feel fun. The two of them discussed plans for a party of some kind.

After a few minutes, the thrill started to wear off. By the end of the conversation, she felt herself getting restless. When they said goodbye, the green line turned red then broke in half.

Nessie waited for another call to come, anxious to get it right, do it faster this time. But time stretched on. She looked around and saw the other operators dutifully pushing the pictures in front of them. It occurred to Nessie that Sandy hadn't told her how to get out. Her heart rate picked up. "Um, sorry, excuse me," she said to Clark. He didn't respond. Nobody did. The infinite black space sprawled out around her and she felt tiny, insignificant. "Hello?!" she called out.

There were shadows out there in the darkness. They weren't like the rest of this other world. They were fluid and sloshed along the corridors, climbing up into tall figures that looked down on her.

Her eyes rolled down and she found herself in the cubicle again. She snatched at her purse and rifled through its contents. She shakily brought a cigarette to her mouth and struggled to keep the lighter's flame lit long enough. Finally she was able to take a deep drag off of it and let out a cloud of relief. Would it always be like that? she wondered. No, she decided, she was letting her mind get carried away. If you stare into a lightless space for long enough, you'll find something there.

As she calmed down, she realized she was in both places at once. It felt like a migraine. But if she quietened her thoughts, she was herself sitting in the cubicle and herself standing in the other space. Simultaneous but independent. She reached out an arm in the real world to ash her cigarette and the other Nessie remained still. Some of the ash fell onto the square Sandy had left in her cubicle. Nessie brushed it away and inspected the label, turning it around in between her fingers, letting it brush the filter of her cigarette.

Nessie looked at the computer and found a slot beside the cassette deck that looked like it might take the square. She tried it one way and it wouldn't go all the way in, so she flipped it and turned it until finally it slipped inside the machine and disappeared behind a tiny door. The computer buzzed and clicked. Nessie was afraid she'd done something wrong, that she'd broken her computer on the first day.

A third self joined the other two and for a brief moment Nessie thought her head might split in two. She fell back against her chair and focused on this newest addition as it demanded her attention. This version was standing beneath towering orange letters that spelled out the word "NEPHILIM". There was a door nestled between the H and the I that was made to look old, weathered, with a ring for a handle. Nessie looked down to find her right hand held a sword and her body was now coated in a knight's dull gray armor. She took a few steps forward and found the door was cracked slightly. The door groaned as she leaned against it. Nessie felt like she had stepped into one of the games from the arcade, Gauntlet or Dragon's Lair.

The swinging door revealed a path of stone, lined by brick walls that held burning torches. The squares making up the flames shifted and broke apart, drifting up and dying. The corridor continued on.

A chittering sound came from the shadows and Nessie felt the weight of fear on her stomach. As she stepped backward, red eyes blinked into existence. She wondered what button she was supposed to press, then remembered there weren't any buttons.

Chunks of the darkness broke free. Stepping into the torchlight, they revealed themselves to be rats, each roughly the size of a dog. Nessie turned back to the door and found it was no longer there. A blank wall of brick greeted her instead.

The rats scurried towards Nessie, their ears laying back against their heads as they became streaks of speed. Nessie shouted and tried to wake herself up again. She could clearly feel herself in the chair, softly snoring. She heard the ringing of the telephone again and tried to focus on it, to pull herself back to the black space and its bright lights. Instead, she saw the operator version of herself instinctively reach out and connect the two pictures, then return to idly standing still, facing forward. Though she could see them, feel them, the brick wall kept her hemmed in.

Nessie heard the rats squeaking to one another. They had formed a semicircle around her, watching her with beady eyes. Their fur was matted with filth, especially around their mouths. One leapt at her, then the others. They were on her in an instant, clawing her face, trying to gnaw through the metal of her armor. Nessie grabbed one, throwing it onto the ground. Without thinking, she drove the sword into its head, feeling the blade slice and crush its way through flesh and bone, finally striking the stone floor on the other side.

The other rats panicked, leaping off of her. She stomped on one of their tails to keep it from getting away, then swung the sword across, lopping off its head. The third scampered off and disappeared. She waited for points to appear or a voice to tell her where to go. If she had known this was going to be a scary game she wouldn't have played it.

Nessie felt something warm on her face. She brought a metal hand to her cheek. Her fingers came away coated with blood.

She blinked hard and realized what she was seeing was no longer made of squares. The red that dripped down to the ground was real. The hallway now reeked of it, from her and the rats. It was enough to make her gag.

After attempting to break through the wall and crying out for help, Nessie accepted that it was futile. The only way out was through, it seemed. Getting a torch from the wall, she held it high as she continued on. This could all be an elaborate dream, she thought. Would that be stranger than having cables plugged into her brain?

Nessie was in a maze of some kind. The torch

seemed to keep the rats at bay for the most part, but there were so many she continually checked behind her. In trying to be alert as possible, she noticed the countless spiders skittering up and along the walls. Their bodies were like black porcelain, reflecting the light of her torch in shining spots along their bulbous bodies. Their webs were dense in places and Nessie was careful to keep the swollen things away from her. She could never be entirely certain they weren't on her, as she continually felt their long needle legs dancing along her neck.

All the walls looked the same. However hard she looked, she couldn't find any distinctive signs that might lead her to the center, or more hopefully, to an exit. She began smudging a trail along her left with the soot from the torch.

It felt like several hours had passed by the time she realized she had circled back to where she had started making marks. Nessie yelled in frustration and threw the torch down a nearby hallway. Her other selves hadn't changed. Eventually the day would be over, right? Someone would come to check on her and realize something was wrong. Yes, of course. She only had to hold out. Struggling to maintain focus, she realized her operator self was still listening to the same phone call. With all her might she was able to force her real eyes open just enough to see that the cigarette was still smoldering between her fingers.

When she came back, Nessie's body had moved within the maze. She turned around and found an enormous set of double doors that stretched up and out of the torchlight. There were symbols Nessie didn't recognize etched into the stone. A lone figure lay in a crumpled heap at the bottom of the door, their armored hand reaching up. The metal of their armor screeched against the stone, which set Nessie's teeth on edge. Their fingers had formed little grooves from countless repetitions.

"Hello?" Nessie called out. The hand stopped as it slapped against the door. Nessie stood still, watching intently. Her mouth went dry and something told her not to call out again. The figure flipped around. A shriek of glee escaped a mangled mouth.. Although his face had changed, like the sagging of melting wax, Nessie recognized the man from the photos in her cubicle. His smile was missing several teeth and only one lens of his glasses was intact. The bushy mustache had spread into a curling crimson beard. He stumbled towards her, arms outstretched. He had taken off most of his armor and piled it beside the door. His hands and legs were covered. The rest of him was bare, save for a tattered cloth around his waist, which held the handle of a sword pressed against his shriveled skin.

"Oh, thank God. Thank God. Please say you're real," he said, getting close.

"Yes, I am," Nessie said, instinctively stepping away from him, putting her hands up.

"Don't be afraid!" he said, smiling. "I'm just so happy to see someone else." His smile did nothing to hide eyes sunken with hunger. "Please. Please come close." Nessie turned slightly, keeping him at a distance. They spun around in the dust until her back was to the door. "Please!" he screamed.

"Listen, mister," Nessie said. "I have no idea what's going on. But maybe we can get out of here."

"Of course!" the man said. "That's all I want. To see my wife and little girl again." Tears cut trails through the dirt on his cheeks. Nessie couldn't tell if he was laughing or crying.

"And we're going to do that," Nessie said, tears of her own forming. The rats and the spiders had not scared her as much as this man with his desperate eyes. "I just need you to calm down so we can think."

The man rushed forward and Nessie shuffled until her back slammed against the door. "I don't want to hurt you!" she said.

The man pulled the jagged edge of a broken sword from his waist and jabbed it at Nessie's face. She batted it away with her own. Despite his frail frame, he grabbed the collar of her armor and tossed her to the ground in a burst of strength. Nessie clumsily tumbled, the weight of the armor dragging her down. Her sword slipped from her hand. "Just hold still," the man said, throwing spit over her as his mouth watered. "It'll be over in just a second." He grabbed Nessie's sword from the ground and held it in both hands. Throwing a leg over the angled chest piece of her armor, he sat down on her belly. Nessie squirmed as he pointed the blade down at her head and brought it up high.

"Get the fuck off me!" she shouted and was able to roll to the side, flipping him onto his back in the dirt. Nessie brought her hands together on the man's throat. She leaned down with all her might. He feebly swung the sword against her side, the armor humming like a bell with a dark tone. A rush of adrenaline ran up Nessie's spine and seemed to flow out of the holes in her skull. The man stopped thrashing and grabbed onto her arms, trying to pry them free.

"Please," the man groaned. But Nessie didn't budge. Her hands ached with how hard she tried to close them completely around his neck. His eyes grew red along with his face, which deepened into a violet blue. Nessie ground her teeth together with the effort, tasting the fragments that were scraped free.

Eventually he was completely still and his eyes became unfocused. She didn't relent.

The grating sound of stone on stone filled the chamber as one of the doors swung inward, revealing more darkness. Exhausted, Nessie finally let go of the man. She struggled to her feet. All she had to do was get through the door. She'd do her job. Get paid. Spend it on whatever she felt like. Right now the thought of a buffet was enough to make her want to weep. She would most definitely report Sandy and this deranged game.

Stepping over the threshold, Nessie no longer felt her other selves. The door shut behind her, leaving her alone in the dark.

Or so she thought.

An orange flame sprang to life in the distance, throwing its light against a white wall. Nessie dragged herself towards it. As she got closer, the flame went higher, leaving the ground and floating up and up along the white wall that fell away in curves, filled with strange shadows.

When Nessie reached where the flame had been, it burned brighter, growing larger. Nessie tripped and fell onto her back as she saw what it was illuminating. A gigantic skull smiled down at her with teeth like concrete slabs. Red rust ran down from a broken crown across its brows, bleeding down into its hollow eyes. The flame flickered as a voice spoke from around and within Nessie.

"Heed my father's words," the voice said. "'Be not afraid. You are worthy.'"

"Please just send me home," Nessie cried out. She clambored to her feet, unable to comprehend what she was looking at. The shadows receded, dripping and

154

sliding away to reveal a full skeleton, seated and leaning back against something Nessie couldn't see. A metal collar hung down against its clavicles. It shifted, sending down a rain of dust and debris.

Nessie ran, but its hand reached out and closed around her body. It lifted her up into the air. Nessie cried out and slammed her fists against the bleached white fingers. A metal manacle about the thing's wrist clanged against its chain like a dozen car crashes echoing off into the nothingness. She squirmed and tried to break free.

Nessie came face to face with the thing.

She felt its empty eyes looking through her, through her memories. Through her soul. It learned everything that made her who she was. It was committing her to memory.

The flame came forward and she felt its heat on her skin. The hand tightened around her and along with the air in her lungs, a small flame came pouring from her mouth. It mingled with the first, coiling and burning brighter. The conjoined flames warmed the armor she was wearing to red hot. She combusted. The flames grew so large they swallowed Nessie entirely. She couldn't scream for the fire's greedy guttering. She smelled burning meat.

Nessie jumped to her feet, her fingers on fire. The cigarette had burned down through the filter and bit her skin. She still felt the thing in her mind, telling her not to fear. Her operator self connected another call.

"You okay?" Sandy asked, peeking over the cubicle wall.

"You!" Nessie said, full of fury. Nessie whipped herself around so fast the cables caught on her chair. She was ready to give Sandy a mouthful when the plugs shifted and the cords yanked free of the ports in her head. It sent a sickening wave of pain down through Nessie's body. She fell face first into the wall and slid to the ground. Her limbs locked in place, but she could see Sandy stepping into her cubicle, standing over her. Nessie tried to speak but her mouth clamped shut. She saw her blood rushing away from her, out into the ash-strewn carpet

Sandy pressed a button and retrieved the Nephilim disk from Nessie's computer. She sucked her teeth in disappointment, looking down on Nessie with something that approached pity.

"So close," Sandy said, waving the disk. "I really thought we had it that time." Clark stood up and craned his neck to see Nessie.

"Damn. Better luck next time," he said. "You sure it isn't getting pissed off?"

"It's just happy to have contact with the real world again. It will get here when it gets here," Sandy said. Sandy crouched down and ran her hand along Nessie's stubbly scalp, shushing her softly. Nessie clung to consciousness as Sandy stood up and started to shout. "Oh my God! Someone help!"

The lights came on as Nessie drifted down into darkness.

"Man! Not again," someone said, exasperated. "How's anybody supposed to get any work done around here?"

"These rookies just can't handle the stress."

DOUBLE EXPOSURE

The night of our senior prom, Kyle was standing next to me on the stairs. I didn't know that, of course, until we had the pictures developed. My dad said it was a "double exposure". He initially didn't want to show me, but he thought it would be for the best. Even if it hurt. The photo wasn't particularly special if you didn't know any better. A little grainy, some bright colored dots floating in the air from the dust. I promise I'm not crazy. I know film does weird, but totally explainable, stuff sometimes.

The Kyle in the picture was not a double exposure.

It was brand new film I watched my mom open and put into the camera, though she came to deny that.

There I was in the photo, standing on the stairs, looking down at my mom, who had some very specific artistic direction she wanted to follow. My suit was too big on my narrow shoulders and I had too much gel in my hair. I was smiling the way I did for mom-enforced shots. The kind she had taken of me and Kyle everytime she took us somewhere.

Behind me, stooping down to place his head on my padded shoulder, was Kyle's face. He was kissing me on the cheek, his lips somewhere between a pucker and a grin. The way he kissed me when no one was looking. When we knew no one else was in the gym, or after our parents had gone to sleep. When I was mad or sad, he would whisper against my neck, something as simple as "Hey,", and it would send chills down over my entire body. I pretended to hate it, but he knew I didn't. "Hey. Hey, what's the matter with the baby?" he'd ask until I laughed so hard I forgot.

The picture did upset me. But in a way I found hard to describe, that I'm still going to struggle with telling you. I felt so guilty when I realized the frantic rush of prom and finals had distracted me from the Kyle-shaped void in my life. The picture was a neon sign in the shape of his silhouette. Like the chalk on the road that had taken weeks to wash away.

In the photo, Kyle looked just like the last time I saw him. It was the end of October then and his cheeks were red from the cold. We had been walking through my neighborhood, admiring the jack-o-lanterns and fake bones scattered across yards that still clung to green life, but were nearly all withered and brown. A big hole opened up in my stomach, knowing he never made it home that night.

I was mad, too. The kind of mad that sends fireworks down your nerves. The anger that would make you try to squeeze blood from a stone and still do it, despite knowing the outcome. There were so many times in those months since it happened that I tried to picture his face. And here it was, here he was, hamming it up in my prom picture. If he were alive, I wouldn't know whether to choke him or kiss him.

The library had a few books on what my mom would call witchcraft in a blanket term pulled from the Satanic Panic handbook. There were histories about the Fox Sisters and seances held around wealthy dining tables. It took me days to find out that none of it was practical, though. I skipped out on plans with the other seniors. The computer lab at school let me look up some webpages. Pixelated images of circles drawn on the floor surrounded by candles. I ate dinner as quickly as possible to avoid talking to my folks.

When graduation came, I posed for every photo my mom wanted me to, urged my mom to use the entire roll. Instead of going to a party, I made her go and get them developed immediately. I was drawn and pale in my black robes and square hat. I could see the hope in my eyes and felt it fizzle out when Kyle was nowhere to be found in the pictures.

I spent the summer trying to make contact. I got a ouija board and a Polaroid camera with my graduation money. It all amounted to nothing, though. I just sat there feeling stupid, my hand on the magnifying glass thing. He didn't have anything to say.

Or maybe I was the problem. Kyle didn't appear in any of the black and white tongues that shot out of the camera. Every once in a while, my door would creak open or a light would dim, and I just knew it was him. His footsteps would come down the hall and stop, my heart thumping and breaking simultaneously. But that was the extent of it.

So in the end, I was left with a stupid board game that I ripped in half and a pile of Polaroids of my room, inside my closet, around the house. All empty. Even on the stairs, trying to recreate the photo of us from prom night. No sign of him. I cried myself to sleep most nights, wondering if he was right there with me and I just couldn't feel him. I couldn't work out what I was doing wrong. There were times I missed him so bad I couldn't breathe. My mom would have to hold me close and rock me like a little kid.

My parents worked out pretty quickly that I hadn't applied to any colleges. They were furious when they confronted me about it. But I had no intention of leaving the house where Kyle's spirit resided. And no intention of telling them that was the case. There was no way I could make them understand.

I told them I was depressed. They sent me to a shrink. A guy with a bad comb-over and an office that smelled like mothballs. Even without telling him about my endeavors to reach Kyle (I really didn't want to be institutionalized), he confirmed what I had been telling them all along. Grief hung around my neck and weighed me down, he said. He said I needed to get more sunshine, more exercise. He gave me pills that put a sealed dome over my brain. I still felt so much, but those emotions never made it past the glass. Mom stood at the sink every morning and made sure I took them. Checked under my tongue and told me it was good for me. At least I didn't cry my eyes out anymore. The nudged cabinets and flickering lights went away, too.

The prom picture went in a drawer with the others of me and Kyle. The therapist suggested this as an "out of sight, out of mind" tactic. He instructed me to look at it one last time and appreciate that a quirk of photography had given us one last snapshot together. The therapist, in his monotone, said to say, "I know this isn't real," out loud. I'd bite my tongue off before I'd say that. But for my parents' sake, I hid us away in the drawer and didn't look while they were home.

All of the pictures were crystal clear in my head, so it didn't do any good for me. They went as far back as kindergarten. Even the most recent felt like I was a little kid. The me that I saw in the mirror now wasn't that happy boy anymore, hugging his friend tight, so tight he'd never be able to go anywhere. My life would forever be separated into with him and without him. I was a skeleton, tired of being upright. I felt like the double exposure, both things at once, the eaten apple core and the ripe fruit it was just moments before.

My dad made me get a job. He said he had lost friends, too. In much worse ways in the war. But you didn't see him moping around. So instead of laying in bed, I stood in a drive-thru for 8 hours at a time, letting my mind wander. In this half-asleep haze, just setting my body through the motions of being a living boy, I stumbled through life until I looked up and realized it was fall. My coworkers tried to make friends with me, but I kept them all at arm's length. They invited me to their party, said I didn't have to dress up if I didn't want to. I said my parents needed me back home. The truth was this: I was the living dead. How could anyone be friends with a mindless monster?

I thought stupid things sometimes.

Like would it be better to check out? Become the actually dead dead? There were a couple different ways I could do it. Maybe Kyle would be waiting for me, so ecstatic I had figured it all out. We could go on and haunt the world until the end of time.

Wouldn't that be nice?

Autumn and Halloween just made me think about him more. His one year anniversary was coming up. How many costumes had we cooked up? How many wrappers were flayed and picked clean over the 12 Halloweens we had had together? Wasn't it Megan's Halloween party in 10th grade when we finally got drunk enough to admit how we felt? Didn't we wander out into the dark, impervious to the chill, and shove each other into piles of leaves? Weren't there still Halloween decorations everywhere when we drove out to the cemetery after his service? Didn't red and orange leaves fall down into the hole that they lowered him into? It was so hard to remember what was real anymore.

When I got home from work, reeking of old oil and a few days without a shower, my parents were gone. They had left a bowl full of candy on the porch that was mostly picked through. I kicked it out into the yard, so angry at being alive. I went in the house and slammed the door. I went upstairs and pulled the pictures out of their drawer, feeling like I was disturbing a holy relic.

Hot tears fell onto the prom picture and I hurriedly swiped them away. With no one in the house, I yelled out loud. I begged him to give me some kind of sign.

I sat in the silence so long it hurt my ears. I looked out my window and saw parents steering their kids away from our porch.

I felt bad and went back out to pick up the candy that I had scattered out into the yard. A shadow came down the driveway. "Sorry, just one second," I said. "I dropped the bowl." I waited for a kid or their parent to say something, but there was no reply. I looked up and didn't see anyone.

I sat down on the porch and watched the sky. The moon was caught in the branches of a tree that had already shed its leaves. I knew it was something Kyle would have appreciated. I missed him. I missed him every day, but in that moment, truly alone and without anyone to monitor my moods, I felt his absence like one might miss a vital organ. "I'm sorry," I said to the night. To him, if he was listening. I knew what I wanted to do and felt so disgusted by it. I buried my face in my hands and tried to push the tears back into my eyes. I took a shuddering breath and let it out as slowly as I could.

I had to give up. On Kyle and ever seeing him again. One day I'd wake up and it wouldn't hurt so bad. One day I'd realize I hadn't thought of him in a while. And I would sit and reminisce.

The hair on my neck bristled and chills ran down my back.

"Hey," a familiar voice whispered from behind me. "What's the matter with the baby?"

OUT THERE

You used to ask me to tell you about the aliens. On the summer nights when we were both lonesome, I'd tell it to you like a ghost story. You'd ask me which star was their home, even though I always told you I had no idea. You knew exactly how the story went and would hear no ad libbed details I tried to sneak in. I don't know if you remember, but we went to The Smithsonian and saw the body they had on display. You cried and cried. Whatever picture you had drawn of them in your mind, the skin and bones beneath the glass did not line up whatsoever. And you didn't want to know more about them after that. But you're grown now, and I'd like to tell you the story again, now that I am a part of it.

When we harvested the crashed ship's engine, we couldn't fathom how it worked. By "we" I mean the collective we; as in all humanity. Eventually we grew up and noticed more of the world around us. I say "noticed", because we have a nasty habit of saying we "discover" things that have been there all along. We couldn't quite crack the code, but in the meantime, we knew with absolute certainty that aliens existed. A ship full of them blinked into existence above the Alps on Christmas Eve, 1946 and ran headlong into one of the peaks. By the time we reached it, the aliens had shriveled into icicle-fringed mummies. People all over the world thought it was a sign of the end times.

On the contrary, it was the beginning of everything.

Scientists from all over the globe came together. Many nations thought this could have been an act of aggression gone awry, so they mobilized forces and united against a common enemy. However, years passed and all that preparation went to waste. We watched the skies for someone that may come looking for their lost citizens, whether they were soldiers, scientists, or pioneers. As far as we could tell, no one had missed them enough to come looking. At the very least, we didn't spend that time fighting each other. Some, myself included, believed these aliens were the last of their kind. They had set out to find a new home and found it, but in the worst way possible.

It was just a few months ago when I was approached by some serious looking people in dark clothes. They asked if I would be interested in joining a voyage to other hospitable planets. The aliens' engine had let us reach the moon, Mars, every other planet that revolved around our sun, but none of them held even the remotest sign of intelligent life. Another function of the engine had been discovered, I was told. One that would allow us to travel anywhere. It was virtually untested. Dangerous. I might never return home, they said. I told them that wasn't much of an issue. I'm sorry I didn't tell you that I was leaving, but it seemed like the right thing to do at the time.

Some dozen planets later, I'm writing to tell you we've failed. Not in the traveling aspect, obviously, but in our main mission. All we've found are remnants, fossilized footprints in the shape of cities.

Each have inspired less and less wonder. The

first we stumbled upon, on Planet 42-Z (the scientists got to name them), caused us to shout and cry with joy. They were made of red stone, plentiful on the supercontinent that covered most of the planet. The doorways were all at least 10 feet tall. The rooms were large, and so we assumed their occupants had been as well. We called out. Only our echoing voices answered. A single member of their civilization greeted us at the heart of the structure. Its bones, not entirely unlike our own, had been scattered about, by a wild animal maybe, or the wind that passed through the doorways in sudden bursts that nearly pushed us down. We left a message of our own, knowing anything that stumbled upon it would have no clue what it meant.

Our most recent endeavor has sent us packing home. We learned the hard way we shouldn't have gone about shouting and drawing attention. Lt. Milo paid the price for that one. He was snatched up by something horrid and dragged off into the sky. We gave chase. While we couldn't retrieve poor Milo, we did stumble upon a wrecked ship. The salty winds coming off the nearby violet ocean had corroded and eaten away at most of the structure. Little things like rats scurried about in the shadows, countless generations born within the ship's rotting metal ribcage.

What I'm about to tell you might not make any sense. You may think I've gone crazy. And maybe I have. Seeing world after world full of nothing but ghosts. Each with homes, businesses, and temples, all standing empty. That aching feeling that if we had been just a day earlier we would have met their occupants. All told, this could cause someone to lose their mind. But I think I've still got most of mine.

I saw myself on that ship. Light Years away from Earth, I stood there breathing, looking down at me. Well, what remained of me. I was the only one left in the marooned ship. The me in the ship clutched a notebook to their chest, covering the patch that bore my name. Most of my suit had decayed, and almost all of my body had been eaten by time or the rat-things. Parts of me had changed. That's all I want to say about that aspect. But it was me. I tried to get my notebook, to find out more, but the others pulled me away. My yawning, smiling skull, stuck in a silent scream, told us to go back.

And so we are. The engine has grown

increasingly strained with each journey. Our rations have run out and we should have just enough juice to jump back home. I'm writing this in case I don't get to tell you in person. Not many people get to look at their desiccated corpse. I may be the only one. Of course it would be wrong to say we discovered me. But it's a feeling I pray no one else has to endure.

I can't make any promises, but if the calculations are correct, we should arrive just before Christmas, if not the day of.

I regret that we are giving up. Maybe someone else will take another voyage like this one. Yes, I think they must. Maybe it will be you. Life exists somewhere out there. I just know it. Beautiful, terrible, intelligent life thrives among the stars, pumps blood or something like it, through bodies ecstatic with the boredom of existence. We need only notice it.

ABOUT THE AUTHOR

Born and raised in Bowling Green, KY, Clinton W. Waters holds a degree in Creative Writing from W.K.U. Their work has been featured in university publications from W.K.U. and the University of Regensburg. They are the lead writer/co-founder of Sundog Comics and their webcomic Variants.

OTHER WORKS
BY CLINTON W. WATERS

-30-

It's Greg's birthday. His 30th birthday. The birthday that
will determine the rest of his life. At midnight, there is
the chance Greg will simply cease to exist. With that in
mind, he has hired Joe, an Ephemera, to accompany
him on what might be his last day on earth. What starts
as a rented relationship soon becomes more
complicated.

Is it possible to fall in love in less than 24 hours? Is
there a point if one of them might not be alive at
midnight?

Greg can only be certain of one thing: the clock is
ticking.

INVERT

In an alternative history 1950s, where atomic war was
waged on the US during World War II, birth rates are

dangerously low. As a result, The Department of Virtue was founded to ensure that not only are people procreating, but they're doing it the right way. The Virtuous Family is a ubiquitous reminder of all that Americans should strive to be.

Greer's life is ruled by the DOV. An invert reformed in one of the nation's many Sanctuaries, he is employed as a "Screw" (Sex Crime Worker). It's his job to entrap other men into making advances so they can be arrested and similarly "reformed". His wife, Alice, is a cured invert as well, prescribed by the state and ordered to attempt procreation. By chance, they have met another invert couple, Bill and Sally. Their romance must remain a secret, or else they may not be given another chance. For Greer, there are eyes in every window and shadows down every side street waiting to catch him slip.

When Greer is assigned Matthews as a new partner, he has to wonder if this man is a plant, meant to keep an eye on him, or if this new Screw is just another victim of Virtue.

Futures Gleaming Darkly

A waiter, strapped for cash, has a watchful AI implanted before work. With a new body, an injured woman is brought face-to-face with trauma from her past. A microchip lets pet owners gain too much insight into their dog's thoughts. In his debut anthology, Futures Gleaming Darkly, Clinton W. Waters offers a window into the human experience in a world that is both mundane and fantastic. Join a host of queer characters as they navigate love, loss, and life in a technology-enhanced not-so-distant future.

A SAMPLE FROM
-30-

Morning

The door creaked open and so did Greg's eyelids. It was blue dawn and socked feet padded their way past his back to the foot of the bed. Greg's phone illuminated his cocoon of comforter, alerting him that his Ephemera, Joe, had arrived. Joe was putting his jacket on the back of the chair at Greg's desk. "Right on time," Greg groaned. They had agreed on the terms of their engagement a few days prior, and Joe was holding true to them. It had felt odd to Greg, giving a stranger the code to get into his apartment. But then again, this was all a little strange.

"You don't get five stars by being late," Joe whispered. Greg could hear the smile in his voice and it made his stomach sweetly sour. How long had it been since someone new was in his bedroom? Leftover dreams clung to the corners of his mind as he rubbed his eyes. When he opened them again, he saw that Joe's stomach was sky blue in the pale light of the morning, his shirt lifting up and over his head. He folded it and draped it over his jacket. His belt buckle clinked as he undid the clasp, jingling as he took off his pants and folded them neatly. He laid them over the back of the chair as well.

Checking the time, Greg did some foggy-brained math and determined he had only gotten a few hours of sleep. Unable to feel tired for the anxiety of it all, he had performed the cardinal sin of trying to do research online, as if that would put his mind at ease. He had done so well up until that point, only the occasional deep dive every few years. He read articles and seriously considered buying some ebooks on the matter. Bombarded by ads for life insurance with sad songs about heaven, he gave up. He wound up at the same conclusion everyone had told him for years. It would never make sense. There would be no correlation. No demographic data that skewed one way or the other. No probability model of lifestyle or location that could give him an honest answer. It all amounted to 50-50.

A coin that had been spinning mid-air for 30 years.

He chuckled to himself at that thought. He was showing his age. Coins. What a novel concept.

Greg sank a little towards the middle of the mattress as Joe sat on the side. "May I join you?" he asked. He turned to look at Greg over his shoulder, which was mottled with pale freckles, tiny hairs glowing as the blue gave way to red and orange. Greg was surprised at how broad Joe was, taller and larger than he had imagined from his pictures on the Ephemera app. He had little love handles that rested above the waistband of his boxers, dark pink stretch marks rising up from below. Greg lifted the comforter and Joe slid in so that they were face to face. The comforter descended again and plunged them into darkness. Just Greg's morning breath mingling with the coffee clinging to Joe's teeth..

"Happy Birthday," Joe said quietly.

"What's so happy about it?" Greg asked, his voice gravelly. He had paid for an entire day. The moment he woke up until just past midnight that night. Had paid extra to ensure midnight was included in their allotted time. From there, whether Greg disappeared or went on living didn't matter. They'd never see each other again. Maybe it never mattered, he thought to himself.

"It's yours, for one," Joe said. He placed a leg over Greg's and pulled up the hem of Greg's shirt, resting his hand on Greg's side. Greg jerked at the cold of it and they both laughed. He felt a bit of the awkwardness ebb away. But this stranger, this Joe was in a spot that had belonged to someone else.

"What about for two?" Greg asked.

"For two, you have me," Joe said into the darkness. Greg's phone illuminated again, a happy birthday text from Avni. Of course she'd be texting him this early. He felt a little silly, but the thought did occur to him that he was excited for her to meet Joe. Maybe that equated to showing Joe off, which didn't make him feel great. But then again, wasn't that a perk of having him in the first place?

Bathed in the dull white glow, Greg begrudgingly admitted to himself how handsome Joe was. How that had been a major factor in choosing which Ephemera he'd spend his 30th birthday with. But more than how attractive he was, Greg felt he "looked" like a boyfriend. The kind who had family out west and had bad taste in music, but called it artistic. Someone to crawl into bed in the wee hours of the morning and stick his cold mitts on your stomach. The kind of guy Greg would take to dinner at his mom's house (an event he would absolutely dread, but Joe would genuinely look forward to). For a moment, the cell phone's light reflected in Joe's dark eyes, and he thought of looking across the table at him and giving him a pained look as his mother veered into politics. He was taking a memory of Zeke and imposing Joe on top of it. It was working perhaps too well.

The light grew dim and shut off, waking Greg up from his daydream.

He thought of the reality. Saying goodbye to his mother the day before. Just in case. Asking her not to come to the party. The pain in her eyes, how her lips grew thin with the effort of biting her tongue. Him bringing up the only other party they had both been at, Alissa's, four years ago.

He took a deep breath and sighed at this.

"And for three, I have the whole day planned out," Joe said, "nothing for you to worry about." This was part of their ruse, however. A line he had given Joe to feed him. Greg had actually planned the entire day, more or less. But Joe was going to handle everything. Carry the bags. Help him decorate for the party. Greg began to think about the party then, his heart beating a little quicker. God, there was so much left to do.

"Hey," Joe said, almost sternly. "Don't spend today worrying, okay?" he said, his hand roving under Greg's shirt. He drew Greg closer to him, his lips finding Greg's in the dark. He kissed him softly, their lips just barely brushing. Greg returned the gesture with force, bringing a hand up to rest on the back of Joe's head. Greg felt as though he should pull away. This was all a lie. A lie he had paid for. But he was ashamed at how quickly his body was ready to accept it, felt starved and wretched. His face grew hot, embarrassed at how pitiful he was. Paying for someone else's company. Joe squeezed him and he said, "Okay?" in a deep grumble.

"Okay," Greg said, relenting and burying his face in Joe's neck. He had the sudden urge to cry. Why not, he figured. He may not have that many opportunities left.

"It will be a good day," Joe said. His arms softened from grip to comforting embrace. "I promise," he whispered. What a way to ruin the mood, Greg thought to himself as he blubbered. But maybe he was a little grateful, a little glad sex wasn't the first thing they did together.

The sun had officially climbed over the horizon by the time Greg's tears ran dry. Joe kissed him on the forehead and slid out of bed. Greg finally emerged from the comforter, eyes red and puffy. "I'm going to get started on breakfast," Joe said, reaching for his clothes.

"Don't," Greg said. Joe smiled and bowed his head slightly. He stood and left. A few moments later Greg heard the clattering of dishes. Greg pulled himself out of bed and stood at his window for a moment. The world outside was well awake by now. Fat flakes of snow were falling lazily from the sky and Greg felt a surge of happiness. He had really been hoping to see snow on his birthday.

If you enjoyed this preview, check out bit.ly/cww30 to find out more!

A SAMPLE FROM
INVERT

The Virtuous Family

Greer sat at a table, waiting for his mark. It was a spooky place and it made him uneasy. Red glass centerpieces with little votive candles threw weird shadows everywhere and cast everything in a bloody hue. Strands of tinsel were strung up, still and glittering in the stagnant, smoke-filled air. Greer had been in plenty of these little hole in the wall places over his four years in the service. But this one gave him the blues. Sad men in a sad place, trying to hide their sad little malediction.

He sat alone, as did all the other men in the bar. A tired lady in a red dress was more or less singing some tune while a skinny man in tight pants and a Santa hat played an equally tired looking piano. She knew she was set dressing. The one woman who kept this place from being an illegal gathering. This tracked. He had noticed they were a skittish bunch. The Surveillance creeps had him coming every couple of nights. What hypocrites, he thought to himself. Perverts watching other perverts. The difference was they had badges and these poor bastards didn't.

He had taken a couple guys for a walk through the nearby alleys. Luckily none of them were brave enough to make a move. He pitied them and their nervous jabber. Their hunger clearly etched in their mournful frowns. Their licked lips. Their tugged groins.

But never an overt physical come on. That's what would get them scooped. The crime was the "committing of an action concurrent with homosexual gratification". The U.S. government and their Department of Virtue hadn't outlawed wanting it. Not yet, anyway. If they had a way to read minds Greer was sure it would be up there with murder.

He was grateful they were triggershy. It wouldn't do for the others to put two and two together. Enough of them go missing or get arrested and they move. Like rats, he thought. Greer needed a specific rodent to take the bait in order to meet his quota. A Mr. Ira Sanderson. Politician type. Not the mayor but someone close. Greer didn't really read the papers.

He took a sip of his whiskey, barely a drop passing his lips. He didn't like to be drunk on the job.

An older fella had been giving Greer the eye for the better part of a half hour. He kept licking his lips like he might eat Greer whole. Looking to the door, Greer was more than halfway relieved to see his target had finally decided to show up. The little bartender had just made last call. His mark was smart. Or at least cautious. He could snag one of these marys as they left. Happen to walk home in the same direction. Plausible deniability.

Greer snubbed most of a good cigarette out, which hurt him. He'd get more in his monthly allotment, but that felt like years away. And it would only come if he got this particular collar. He made eye contact with Sanderson, who had yet to take off his coat. Good, he was in a hurry too.

Kicking his chair back softly, Greer stood. He threw some change on the table. He kept his eyes trained on Sanderson's as he stepped towards the door. So far so good. The "singer" was packing it in and the pianist was lowering the key cover.

Sanderson took a step, trying to get out of Greer's way. Greer got close instead, reaching over Sanderson's shoulder to get his coat. He had to be careful. If he was the first to initiate touch, it would all be worthless. The red light and his thin mustache made Sanderson look like a devil from the cartoons. Come to tempt a man into a sinful act. Greer winked. Sanderson smiled.

Greer went through the door, into the cold night. He made it up the stairs to street level before he looked back. Sanderson stood in the doorway watching him. Greer tilted his head back. Sanderson started up the stairs.

Greer walked along the road for a minute. He stopped and Sanderson stopped too, about six feet back. Greer feigned having trouble keeping a match lit long enough to light his cigarette. Sanderson swooped in. He flicked a gold lighter into life and held it beneath the cigarette's tip. His teeth were orange in the fire's light. Greer thanked him.

Sanderson started walking down a nearby alley. Damn. Greer wasn't leading the dance anymore. But no matter. Whatever this guy needed to feel comfortable enough to kiss or touch him. Greer followed Sanderson for a bit, careful to keep a map in his head of how to get back to the street in case things went sideways.

He turned a corner and found Sanderson in a dead end, surrounded by garbage cans and darkness. This was it. "What's your name?" Sanderson asked with a grin. Greer gave him something. "I like that," Sanderson said as he undid the button on his pants. "Come here," he said. Greer looked around, playing scared. He used that time to ensure an officer had followed them. Sure enough, he saw Jenkins creeping towards him. "No one will find out," Sanderson whispered. Greer smiled and moved close. Careful. Don't touch him. Sanderson pushed his pants down and Greer swallowed, trying not to look down. "It's all right," Sanderson said quietly. Sanderson grabbed Greer's hand and put it on his crotch. Greer felt the warmth and screwed his eyes shut tight. Bile-diffused whiskey came up in the back of his throat.

"Hands up!" Jenkins yelled from behind Greer. Greer complied immediately, backing away. Someone from Surveillance was there, snapping pictures. Sanderson floundered, trying to yank his pants up. Jenkins "arrested" Greer first. He pushed him into the nearby brick wall and mashed his face against it. His cheek burned as the brick bit into it. When he got apprehended along with his marks, he found every beatwalker did it differently. None of them were his friends, wouldn't be. But there were assholes like Jenkins who enjoyed making it more painful than it had to be. "It's gotta be believable," he said the last time Greer confronted him about it. He had also spat a wad of phlegm at his feet for extra measure.

"We'll be taking you both in for questioning," Jenkins said, wrapping the cuffs around Sanderson's wrists. He was spluttering. Saying how they didn't have to do this. He had been a friend to the police department for many years. "Save it for the judge," Jenkins said, yanking Sanderson forward, then peeling Greer off the wall.

They rode in the back of the police car in total silence. Greer hazarded a single glance at Sanderson, but the man was distraught. "I'm sorry," he finally said, tears streaming down his face. "I got you mixed up in all this." Greer was stunned. Over the years, his fake arrests did their job of putting up appearances, in case his collars went on to blab. But none of them had ever apologized to him. "My wife is going to kill me," Sanderson said to himself. Greer watched him press his forehead to the window and let out a whimper. It made Greer's lip curl in disgust.

No, Greer thought. You won't die. You may wish you had at some point. But the Sanctuaries had a way of turning you around. Making sure your insides matched your outsides. You just had to survive until you got to that point. Sanderson being married already would help. Greer didn't know if he had a child, but if they had managed to conceive at some point, all the better. He'll be just fine, Greer thought to himself.

Once inside the precinct, they were led to separate rooms. Greer's handcuffs were removed and he jotted down some information in a log book. The officer on desk duty that night wouldn't look at him. "Have a good one," Greer said, feeling like being an asshole. The officer pretended not to hear, slamming the log book closed and taking it off to wherever it lived. He muttered, the only thing Greer catching for certain was "invert".

Greer stepped out onto the street. The cold wind on his inflamed face felt good. He touched the wound and his fingers came away with just a little bit of blood. He'd had worse. He took his time getting to the DOV. Once inside, the night clerk looked over his badge before letting him through another set of interior doors. As if the man hadn't seen him come in countless times.

The place was clean in a gross way. Like a church or a hospital. How meticulously some people had to work to make this place look this good. He paused to look at the mural that took up the entire back wall. You could see it from the street, but no one would really need to. Their posters and ads in the newspapers used it, and images like it, over and over again. They prescribed what every citizen should strive for. Men worked, stoic guardians of their home and country. Women served and created happy homes. They both were expected to create more Americans, to ensure these virtues were passed on and propagated.

A man and woman stood, admiring the stars and stripes. The man had an arm around his wife's shoulder. She nestled into him, each of her arms draped over the shoulders of their children. A little boy, dressed like a soldier. He stood in present arms, a rifle strapped to his back, his hand hovering below his oversized helmet in a perpetual salute. The little girl looked hopeful, hugging a rag doll to her chest. Their white skin (for what other color could it be?), their light hair, stood out in the darkness of the lobby after hours. Lit from below, they looked like ghouls to Greer. Ghosts of war. Pale corpses held up and trotted about.

While Greer hated them, was tired of this fictional family rearing their ugly heads, he envied them. Their existence was uncomplicated, he imagined. They loved each other, and their country. He gave them all the middle finger before stepping away. Greer took the stairs down to the basement, where the Sex and Gender Divison was housed.

Made in the USA
Middletown, DE
03 September 2024

60263036R00116